'All ready?' Nico asked, walking over to them.

His gaze skimmed over her, taking stock of the coral-pink dress she had chosen to wear. Although it wasn't an expensive designer number it suited Amy, he decided, the colour setting off her soft brown hair and adding a glow to her lightly tanned skin.

She looked so young and so lovely as she stood there holding Jacob's hand that he was overwhelmed by a sudden need to touch her. Bending, he kissed her on the cheek, his lips lingering on her warm, sweet-smelling skin as a host of emotions flowed through him.

He cared about her and there was no point pretending that he didn't. He cared about her and, what was more, he always had.

Dear Reader,

The idea for *The Greek Doctor's Secret Son* came to me a couple of years ago, after I had enjoyed a wonderful holiday in the Greek Islands. I decided it would be the ideal setting for my next book, and soon came up with a story and characters who seemed absolutely perfect.

I set about writing Amy and Nico's story with great enthusiasm, only to find halfway through their tale that I had reached a dead end. I simply didn't know where I was heading, or how to do justice to the characters I had created, so I set the book aside and wrote something else. However, at the back of my mind Amy and Nico kept niggling away, demanding that their story should be told.

I returned to the book earlier this year, and lo and behold everything suddenly slotted into place. Some books just need that extra bit of time to allow the characters and their story to develop. This book was one of them!

Best wishes to you all,

Jennifer

To learn more about the setting for this book please visit my blog: jennifertaylorauthor.wordpress.com.

THE GREEK DOCTOR'S SECRET SON

BY
JENNIFER TAYLOR

First published in Great Britain 2016 20404996
By Mills & Boon, an imprint of HarperCollins*Publishers*
1 London Bridge Street, London, SE1 9GF

Large Print edition 2016

© 2016 Jennifer Taylor

ISBN: 978-0-263-26126-4

Our policy is to use papers that are natural, renewable
and recyclable products and made from wood grown
in sustainable forests. The logging and manufacturing
processes conform to the legal environmental
regulations of the country of origin.

Printed and bound in Great Britain
by CPI Antony Rowe, Chippenham, Wiltshire

Jennifer Taylor has written for several different Mills & Boon series, but it wasn't until she 'discovered' Medical Romances that she found her true niche. Jennifer loves the blend of modern romance and exciting medical drama. Widowed, she divides her time between homes in Lancashire and the Lake District. Her hobbies include reading, walking, travelling and spending time with her two gorgeous grandchildren.

Books by Jennifer Taylor

Mills & Boon Medical Romance

The Doctor's Baby Bombshell
The Midwife's Christmas Miracle
Small Town Marriage Miracle
Gina's Little Secret
The Family Who Made Him Whole
The Son that Changed his Life
The Rebel Who Loved Her
The Motherhood Mix-Up
Mr Right All Along
Saving His Little Miracle
One More Night with Her Desert Prince...
Best Friend to Perfect Bride
Miracle Under the Mistletoe

Visit the Author Profile page
at millsandboon.co.uk for more titles.

CHAPTER ONE

IT HAD SEEMED like such a good idea back home in England. Now she wasn't so certain any more. What if something went wrong, something she hadn't foreseen? She could end up creating even more problems if she weren't careful.

Amy Prentice could feel her anxiety mounting as she and her eight-year-old son, Jacob, joined the queue for the ferry that would transport them to the small Greek island of Constantis. It had all appeared so straightforward when they had set off that morning. She would take Jacob to Constantis for a holiday and whilst they were there, she would tell him about his father being Greek. At the moment Jacob knew very little about the man who had fathered him apart from the fact that he was a doctor and that he worked in America, which was why they never saw him. Jacob had accepted it without question, or he had done before the other children in his class had started teasing him. Although a lot of them came from single-parent families too, at least they had some contact with their absent parent. Jacob, however, had never met his father and that was all down to her.

Nicolaus Leonides had made his feelings abundantly clear nine years ago. He hadn't been interested in the child Amy had been carrying and there was no reason to imagine that he had changed his mind. Not after everything she had read about him. Nico had achieved everything he had set out to do, establishing himself as one of the world's foremost cosmetic surgeons. The name Nicolaus Leonides had become a byword for perfection and the fact that only those with a great deal of money could afford to be treated at his clinic in California was immaterial.

No, Nico wouldn't be interested in Jacob's problems even if she was prepared to contact him, which she had no intention of doing. Staying on the island where Nico had spent so much time when he was growing up had been the best way Amy could think of to give Jacob an idea of his paternal heritage. So why did she feel so unsure all of a sudden, so afraid that she might be opening up a whole new can of worms? She hung back, the weight of the suitcase dragging painfully on her arm as she debated the pros and cons of carrying on with her plan. Jacob had already skipped up the gangplank but he stopped when he realised that she wasn't following him.

'Come on, Mum! You're going to miss the ferry if you don't hurry up!'

Amy sighed when she heard the excitement in his voice. Coming on this trip had given Jacob a much-needed boost and it was good to hear him sounding so upbeat for a change. He would be bitterly disappointed if she announced that they were no longer going to the island. She worked such long hours in her job as senior sister on the acute assessment unit at Dalverston General Hospital and saw far too little of him. This trip had been a chance to redress the balance as much as anything else.

Amy took a deep breath then hefted their suitcase up the gangplank. She couldn't give up now that they had come this far. And as for creating problems, well, there was no basis for thinking that. After all, there was no danger of them running into Nico. He was thousands of miles away, adding even more dollars to his bulging coffers!

Nico broke into a run. The last passengers had already boarded the ferry and the crew were preparing to cast off. If he missed this boat there wouldn't be another one until the following day and he couldn't afford to stay on the mainland overnight. There was an open surgery in the morning which was always packed full of people requiring his attention and he couldn't let them down.

He put on a final spurt and just managed to leap aboard as the crew cast off the final rope. He nodded apologetically when one of the older men remonstrated with him. Maybe he shouldn't have taken such a risk but it felt good to know that he was fit enough to push himself like that. When he'd had that heart attack three years ago, he had honestly thought that was it, that all he could expect from then on was a sedentary existence. It had taken him a while to adjust to the idea of his own mortality but once he had done so, he had realised that he could still enjoy life so long as he was sensible about it.

He had set about making changes to the way he had lived, starting with the biggest issue of all, the amount of stress he was under. Setting up the practice in California and making it a success had been his *raison d'être*. He had worked eighteen-hour days and then spent any free time networking; however his cardiologist had made it clear that he couldn't do that any longer. Not if he wanted to avoid another heart attack.

He had sold the practice and moved back to Greece, taken a year out while he worked out what he wanted to do with the rest of his life. It had been hard to imagine doing anything other than what he had devoted himself to for the best part of twenty years and he had struggled to find a new direction. And then one day he had taken a trip to Constantis, the tiny island where he and his sister had enjoyed so many holidays with their grandparents, and he had realised in amazement that he had wanted to live there.

There had been no medical facilities on the island at the time. If anyone was taken ill, they had to be ferried to the mainland for treatment. Nico had contacted the IKA, the body which ran the Greek health service, and they had been cautiously enthusiastic about his proposal to build a clinic providing primary health care as well as a ten-bed hospital unit. It had taken a lot of negotiation but in the end he had been given the go-ahead, mainly, he suspected, because he had been willing to fund the building costs himself. The Ariana Leonides Clinic had been open for twelve months now and it was thriving.

Nico moved further along the deck, smiling as

he passed several people he knew. Although he had a staff of ten working with him at the clinic, he was well known to the islanders and he had to admit that he enjoyed that aspect of the job too. Although he had led a busy social life in California, he had been aware that the invitations had been extended because of his status more than anything else. His name on a guest list had been seen as real kudos by the hostess, something to brag about. He was rich, successful and that was what had mattered most of all.

A sudden commotion made him glance round and he frowned when he saw a crowd starting to gather near the railings. Forcing his way through it, he spotted a girl lying on the deck. She was obviously a tourist from her clothing—tiny denim shorts and an equally skimpy top—and she appeared to be unconscious. There was a young man kneeling beside her and he looked up in panic when Nico approached.

'I don't know what happened. One minute she

was taking photos with her phone and the next second she just collapsed!'

'Does she have a history of fainting?' Nico asked, crouching down beside the girl.

'I don't know! We only met a couple of days ago so I have no idea if this is something she does regularly,' the young man explained.

'I see. What's her name?' Nico asked, checking the girl's pulse which was extremely rapid.

'Jane.' The boy gulped. 'She's from Australia although I don't know where exactly. As I said, I only met her a couple of days ago and we've spent most of the time since then partying.'

Nico sighed. *Partying* implied that the young couple had been drinking and maybe even taking drugs. He had dealt with several such cases recently and the most difficult task of all was getting the youngsters to admit what they had taken so they could receive the appropriate treatment. He stood up and drew the boy aside so they could speak in private.

'Has she taken something? I'm a doctor and

you need to tell me if she has taken any drugs or I can't help her.'

'No, no! It's nothing like that,' the young man protested but Nico could tell he was lying.

His tone hardened. 'This isn't the time to worry about your own skin. If Jane has taken drugs then I need to know what I'm dealing with. To put it bluntly, she could die if she doesn't receive the appropriate treatment.'

'I don't know anything about any drugs!' the young man claimed. He suddenly spun round, forcing his way through the crowd and disappearing from sight.

Nico cursed under his breath as he knelt down beside the girl again. He couldn't afford to go after him when he needed to stay here. He rolled her onto her side, working on the assumption that she had taken some kind of narcotic and could start vomiting. She was burning hot and her breathing was shallow which all supported his theory that an overdose of drugs was to blame for her collapse. The problem was finding out exactly what she had taken.

'My mummy's a nurse,' piped up a small voice. 'She can help make the lady better—shall I get her?'

Nico glanced up and saw a boy of about eight years of age watching him. He had light brown hair and dark brown eyes and for some reason he looked strangely familiar... He blanked out the thought and smiled at the child. It would be a huge help if he had someone to assist him, especially if Jane's heart stopped beating, as could very well happen.

'Yes, please. I could do with an extra pair of hands.'

The child nodded gravely then hurried away. Nico turned back to the girl, checking her pulse once more as well as her breathing. Neither seemed to have improved but there again they didn't seem to have got any worse either which was something to be grateful for.

'Jacob said you needed help.'

The clear tones cut through the babble of voices and Nico felt his heart come to a dead stop. He looked up, squinting against the glare of the sun. It couldn't be her, he told himself, his gaze resting on the slender figure standing over him, not here, not now, not on this ferry. It was too big a coincidence to imagine that fate had brought them together after all this time.

'You!'

The word exploded from her lips yet she hadn't shouted; it was said so quietly, in fact, that only he could have heard her. Nico rose to his feet, his breath coming in laboured spurts as he tried to make sense of what was happening. He regretted very little that had happened in his life simply because he had worked out what he had wanted and how he would achieve it too. Every decision he had made had been thought through and deliberated upon. Except one. He had never planned for her to get pregnant.

'Amy.'

Her name flowed so easily from his lips that

it shocked him all over again. It was years since
he had seen her and yet there was no hesitation
about recalling who she was. His eyes skimmed
over her, taking stock of the light brown hair fall-
ing to her shoulders, the brilliant gleam of her
green eyes, the slender curves of her body. She
didn't look a day older than the last time he had
seen her, he realised in amazement. It was hard
to believe that all those years had passed…

'Do you know what's wrong with her?'

The abruptness of the question brought him
back to earth with a bump. Nico crouched down
beside the girl again, doing his best to steer his
thoughts in the direction they needed to go. He
had a patient who required his help and this
wasn't the time to start thinking about how much
he regretted what had gone on between him and
Amy Prentice.

'I suspect it may be a drug overdose,' he said,
relieved that he was still able to function on a
professional level. He nodded towards the girl's
backpack. 'Can you take a look in there and see

if there's anything that may give us a clue as to exactly what she's taken?'

'Of course.'

Amy knelt down and unzipped the bag, trying her best not to let him see that her hands were shaking. Meeting Nico like this had been a massive shock and she could feel the aftermath of it rippling through her like a series of seismic explosions. It was difficult to maintain her control but she had to do so for Jacob's sake. There was no way on this earth that she wanted her son to guess that this man was his father!

A moan slid from her lips and she hurriedly turned it into a cough when she saw Nico glance at her. She turned away, focusing on the contents of the girl's bag. There were all the usual items: T-shirts, underwear, toiletries. And then right at the bottom, tucked into a corner, she found what they were looking for. Holding up the small glass bottle, she showed it to Nico.

'GBL if I'm not mistaken. The bottle's half full

though there's no way of knowing how much she's taken today.'

'Right.' Nico's tone was grim. 'At least we know what we're dealing with although that doesn't guarantee that we'll be able to help her.'

Amy nodded. Gammabutyrolactone, GBL for short, had become increasingly popular with the student population. Even a small dose could have a powerful sedative effect and if mixed with alcohol could be extremely dangerous, often leading to unconsciousness or even death. The girl would need immediate treatment if she was to have any chance of pulling through.

'What's that, Mummy? Is it medicine to make the lady better?'

Amy tried not to show her dismay that Jacob was witness to what had happened. He was only eight and she wanted to protect him from things like this for as long as possible. She opened her mouth to explain that it was nothing for him to worry about but Nico beat her to it.

'It's not medicine. Medicine makes people better but this is something very different,' he explained quietly. 'Something she shouldn't have taken.'

'Oh, you mean drugs.' Jacob nodded sagely. 'They told us about them in school. I don't know why anyone wants to take them when they make them ill, do you?'

'No, I don't.'

Nico smiled up at the boy and Amy felt her heart turn over in fear. The resemblance between them at that moment was so marked that she couldn't believe Nico hadn't noticed it. Although Jacob had her colour hair, he had inherited Nico's olive skin and chestnut-brown eyes. Even his nose was a smaller, childish version of Nico's, arrow straight without even the hint of a tilt to it. It was all she could do not to whisk Jacob away and hide him so that Nico would never guess he was his son. After all, he didn't deserve a son like Jacob, did he? Not after what he had said when she had suffered that miscarriage.

It's for the best, he had stated coldly when she

had told him that she had lost the baby. They had never planned on having a child and the fact that she had lost it made things simpler.

Even though Amy had known from the outset that Nico hadn't been overjoyed when she had realised that she was pregnant, she had been deeply hurt. They had met at the hospital where Amy was completing her nursing degree. She was in her final year while Nico was on the exchange programme. The hospital was a centre of excellence in the field of plastic surgery and Nico had taken up the offer of a consultant's post there.

They had both attended a fundraising event one evening. It had been very well supported and the room had been crowded. She had, quite literally, bumped into him and managed to spill her drink all down the front of his jacket. She had been absolutely mortified but Nico had taken it remarkably well, brushing aside her apologies and insisting on fetching her another drink. They had got talking and one thing had led to another; he had asked her out for dinner, she had accepted.

After a couple of months, she had been more than a little in love with him and had thought—hoped!—that he had felt the same way. However, his reaction first to her pregnancy and then to the miscarriage had soon put paid to that idea. Amy had realised that all she had ever been to him was a pleasant little interlude, someone to spend time with while he was in London, someone to sleep with. He definitely didn't want to tie himself to her with or without a child.

That was why she had ended their relationship. She simply couldn't bear to carry on seeing him, knowing how he really felt about her. It was also the reason why she had decided not to tell him when she had discovered a couple of months later that she was still pregnant, that she must have been carrying twins and had miscarried only one of them. Nico had finished his stint on the exchange programme by then and had left London and moved to Los Angeles to further hone his skills. Although she could have tracked him down if she had wanted to, there hadn't seemed any point. Nico hadn't wanted her or their child, and he had made it clear.

He probably still wouldn't want them now either, Amy thought bitterly. Which meant that she would need to be very careful. Maybe she had coped with having her heart broken but she wouldn't allow the same thing to happen to Jacob. She took a deep breath. She couldn't afford to panic, not when she had to make sure that Nico didn't find out that Jacob was his son!

CHAPTER TWO

NICO USED THE ferry's radio to contact the clinic so an ambulance was waiting when they docked at Constantis's tiny, picturesque harbour. He supervised the transfer himself, wanting to get the girl back to the clinic as quickly as possible. She was still unconscious and the longer she remained so, the greater the risk that she might not recover.

Once the ambulance was on its way he went to fetch his car, pausing when he saw Amy and the child disembarking. He couldn't just drive off without speaking to her, could he? Even if they had been total strangers, at the very least he would have to thank her for helping him, and they were a long way from being strangers. Heat poured through his veins as he found himself recalling the time they had spent together in London. Even though it was years ago, he could remember only too clearly how he had felt when they had made love. Amy had touched him in ways that no woman had ever done.

The thought shocked him, unsettled him, made him feel all sorts of things, and that was another first. He had learned to contain his emotions at an early age and preferred to keep his feelings under wraps. To find himself feeling so churned up wasn't a pleasant experience and he did his best to get a grip. Maybe Amy had aroused feelings he had never experienced before or since but that was all in the past and a lot had happened in the interim. His gaze moved to the boy at her side and his mouth thinned. How old was he? Eight? Nine? Whichever it was, the child was proof that Amy hadn't wasted any time getting over him.

That thought accompanied him as he made his way over to them. He forced himself to smile even though it wasn't as easy as it should have been. The realisation that Amy had found someone to replace him so quickly didn't sit comfortably with him, funnily enough. He found himself recalling her distress when she had suffered that miscarriage and frowned. Had that been a key factor? Had she felt the need to replace not only him but the child she had lost? It made a certain kind of sense and yet he couldn't quite believe it. Amy had never struck him as the kind of woman who moved from one man to another without a great deal of thought.

'Thank you for your help,' he said formally, determined to get back on track. All this soul searching was unsettling and he needed to call a halt. He glanced at the suitcase at her feet. 'I take it that you are staying on the island?'

'That's right. We're staying at the Hotel Marina, right on the beach. We're really looking forward to it, aren't we, Jake?' She smiled at the child although Nico saw a flash of something that looked almost like fear cross her face.

'I'm sure you will enjoy it,' he said politely, wondering what had caused it. He brushed aside the thought, determined that he wasn't going to be sidetracked. 'My sister and I spent many happy holidays here with our grandparents when we were children.'

'Is that why you're here now?' she said quickly. 'For a holiday?'

'No. I opened a clinic on the island twelve months ago and I live here now.'

'Really?'

'Yes.' He shrugged. 'I'm very fortunate to live and work in such a beautiful place.'

'You are, although I don't imagine that was the main reason you set up a clinic here.' She gave a soft little laugh and Nico felt his skin prickle when he heard the contempt it held. 'No doubt it's the ideal place to tap into the lucrative European market. There's a huge demand for cosmetic surgery procedures from across the whole of Europe, I believe, and travelling to Greece must be a lot quicker than travelling to the USA.'

'The Ariana Leonides Clinic doesn't offer cosmetic surgery procedures. Its aim is to provide primary health care for locals and tourists.' He shrugged when he saw from her expression that he had surprised her. For some reason he couldn't explain, he knew that he wanted to set matters straight. 'There's also a ten-bed hospital unit for minor surgery cases.'

'I had no idea…' She broke off and shrugged. 'It all sounds very different from what I would have expected, but there again it's been a long time since I saw you, Nico. There's bound to have been changes in your life.'

'In yours too,' he agreed, looking pointedly at the child standing beside her.

'Indeed.' She gave him a brief smile but once again he saw that flash of fear cross her face and it intrigued him. It was on the tip of his tongue to ask her what was wrong when she picked up her suitcase. 'Anyway, I won't keep you. I'm sure you must be anxious to check how your patient is doing. It was nice to see you again, Nico. Take care.'

With that, she made her way to the taxi rank.

There were only three taxis on the island and as luck would have it, there happened to be one free. Nico watched her hand her case to Aristotle, the driver, then usher the boy into the back of the cab. It roared away in a cloud of exhaust fumes, leaving him wishing that he had said something, done something, at least made arrangements for them to meet again. Even though he knew it was crazy, he couldn't help feeling, well, *bereft* as he watched the taxi disappear around the headland…

Nico shook his head to rid himself of that foolish notion. Going over to his car, he got in and started the engine. He had everything he needed *and* wanted. He had made up his mind a long time ago that he would never commit himself to a relationship. He was too much like his father to take that risk. Maybe he had made a lot of changes to his life since his heart attack, but, basically, he was still the same person he had always been. One couldn't escape one's genes, after all. No, getting involved with Amy was out of the question even if she had been willing, which he very much doubted.

As for having a family, well, that was another non-starter. To put it bluntly, he refused to subject any child to the kind of upbringing he'd had. That was why he had been so dismayed when Amy had announced that she was pregnant. He had kept thinking about his own childhood, remembering how he had felt growing up as the son of Christos Leonides. Although his father might be revered by the business community even today, few people knew what he was really like.

Christos Leonides was a cold and ruthless man who had always put his business interests first and had cared nothing for his wife and his children. While neither Nico nor his sister, Electra, had been physically mistreated when they were growing up, they still bore the mental scars of their father's indifference. Their mother had done her best while she'd been alive to compensate for it but it had had a lasting effect on both of them, especially on Nico. Although Electra seemed to have come to terms with the past since she had married and had her own family, Nico had been unable to rid himself of the fear that he would turn out exactly the same as his father.

That was why he had ruled out the idea of having children and why it had been a relief when Amy had miscarried their baby, even though part of him had grieved for their lost child. He had been so shaken when he had realised it too that he had buried his feelings beneath a veneer of disinterest and it didn't make him feel good to know that he had hurt Amy. Badly. She had suffered one of the worst experiences any woman could go through and he had made it so much worse by pretending that he hadn't cared.

Nico's heart was heavy as he set off for the clinic. He didn't regret many things in his life, but he regretted that.

Amy finished unpacking and stowed the suitcase in the corner out of the way. Glancing around the small, whitewashed bedroom, she felt some of the tension start to seep out of her. Meeting Nico had been a shock but the upside was that she had got through the experience relatively unscathed. She had often wondered how she would react if they met again, but surprisingly she didn't feel much different from normal. Although her heart was beating a shade faster than usual, it certainly wasn't racing, and her breathing was only the tiniest bit laboured. She was functioning perfectly well and if that wasn't proof that she was over him then she had no idea what was.

'Can we go to the beach now, Mum?'

Amy glanced round when Jacob came racing into the room. She had allowed him to explore the small hotel where they were staying while she unpacked, although he had been under strict instructions not to leave the building. Now she smiled at him. 'I can't see why not. Do you want to put your swimming trunks on? We may as well have a swim while we're at it.'

'Yes!' Jacob punched the air in delight as he

ran over to the wardrobe and took out his swimming trunks. Stripping off his clothes, he put them on and raced towards the door.

'Hold it right there, young man.' Amy picked up the bottle of sunscreen, ignoring his grimace as she started to apply it to his skin. 'There's no point pulling a face. I told you before we came here that you have to use sunscreen before you go outside. The sun is a lot hotter here than it is at home and you don't want to get burned, do you?'

'I bet *he* doesn't wear sunscreen,' Jacob muttered, screwing up his face as she applied a layer of cream to his nose.

'Who doesn't?' Amy asked, busily rubbing it in.

'The man on the ferry, that doctor—Nico, you called him.' Jacob tilted his head to the side and looked questioningly at her. 'How come you knew his name, Mum? He knew yours too 'cos he called you Amy, so have you met him before?'

'I…erm… Yes. But it was a long time ago.' Amy screwed the top back on the bottle, feeling her hands trembling. She had forgotten how observant Jacob was and she should have realised that he would pick up on something like that.

'Where did you meet him? I thought you said that you hadn't been to this island before,' Jacob continued, making it clear that he didn't intend to let the subject drop.

'I haven't.' Amy picked up her beach bag, making a great production out of checking that she had everything they needed: towels, sunglasses, water…

'So you met him somewhere else?' Jacob persisted. 'Was it at the hospital? Did he used to work in Dalverston?'

'Not Dalverston, no. We met in London while I was studying to be a nurse,' Amy explained, hoping that would satisfy him.

'London? That's where you met my daddy, wasn't it? Does he know him?' Jacob's voice was filled with excitement. 'Maybe he has some photos of my daddy or knows where he lives. Can we ask him, Mum? *Please!*'

'Jacob, stop it! Nico—I mean that man—doesn't know anything about your daddy.' Amy took a deep breath, struggling to stay calm, but it wasn't easy. Maybe it wasn't a total lie; after all Nico had no idea that he was Jacob's father. Nevertheless, it didn't make her feel good to have to fudge the truth and she hurriedly changed the subject. 'Now come along. No more questions. Let's go and have that swim. Last one in the water is a lazy monkey!'

Jacob responded to the challenge as she had hoped he would, racing out to the terrace that led onto the garden. Amy followed more slowly, needing to get herself together so that he wouldn't suspect anything was amiss. She sighed. Jacob had become increasingly curious about his father since the other children had started teasing him and it was only to be expected when he knew so little about him. Jacob had never seen a photograph of Nico, never been told anything about his father's background, and it was all her doing too.

She had blanked out that period in her life because it had been too painful to think about it. However, she couldn't continue blanking it out, certainly couldn't refuse to answer Jacob's questions for ever. At some point she would have to tell him about the man who had fathered him, which was why she had decided to bring him to Constantis. Giving Jacob a sense of his true identity was the first step, she had reasoned, and the rest would follow later. However, she was very aware that things might happen sooner than she had anticipated now that Nico was on the scene. Should she get it all over and done with? she wondered suddenly. Tell Nico who Jacob was and then tell *Jacob* that Nico was his father?

Amy immediately dismissed the idea. She couldn't tell Jacob that Nico was his father until she was sure of Nico's reaction and even then she might have to keep the truth from him. After all, there was no reason to believe that Nico would welcome the news that he had a son, was there? The one thing she wouldn't risk was Jacob getting hurt if Nico rejected him, as he might very well do.

* * *

'We'll keep her here overnight. She may need to be transferred to the mainland tomorrow but it's too risky to move her at the moment. Can you keep an eye on her, please? She may have recovered consciousness but she's not out of the woods yet.'

Nico smiled his thanks when Sophia nodded. As acting sister on the hospital unit, Sophia Papadopolous had proved her capabilities more than once. He was planning on making her position permanent and only hoped that she would agree. Sophia had returned to Constantis after a long stint of working in Italy. Although she hadn't said anything to him, he had heard via the clinic's redoubtable grapevine that she had returned following the break-up of a relationship. Sophia had been disappointed in love and had come home whereas he had come here for the good of his health. Everyone had their reasons for being on the island, it seemed, even Amy. Had she come here simply for a holiday?

Or had there been another reason for her visit? From what she had said, she'd had no idea that he was living here so that couldn't have been a factor and yet it seemed strange that she should have chosen this island rather than one of the more popular tourist destinations.

He tried to dismiss the unsettling thought as he went to his office and put through a call to the Australian Embassy in Athens. He had found Jane's passport tucked into the pocket of her haversack and now had her full name and address. He spoke to one of the attachés who promised to contact the girl's parents. According to her passport, Jane Chivers was eighteen years of age and although legally an adult, Nico guessed that her parents would want to know what had happened to her. In their shoes, he would have done.

Nico frowned as he ended the call. It was the kind of thought that would never have occurred to him before and yet it had appeared, fully fledged, in his mind. Why? Had it anything to do with meeting Amy and her son? Had it somehow triggered a reaction to see the boy and wonder what would have happened if she hadn't lost their baby? He sensed it was true and it alarmed him. He didn't want to go down that route. It was pointless. Pointless and strangely upsetting too.

Nico left his office and went to check that there was nothing that needed his attention before he went home. There had been an antenatal clinic that afternoon but Elena Delmartes, one of their most experienced doctors, had dealt with it and there had been no problems. Offering a comprehensive health care package to the islanders had been his aim when he had set up the clinic and he knew that the women appreciated not having to travel to the mainland for their antenatal care. Although most still preferred to have their babies delivered at home by the local midwives, they came to the clinic for their check-ups. It was a system that worked extremely well. According to the latest figures, very few women had missed an appointment at the clinic which certainly hadn't been the case when they had needed to travel to the mainland. It meant that every baby born on the island had an increased chance of being born healthy.

He drove home, taking his time as he travelled along the familiar route. Once his proposal for the clinic had been given the green light, he had set about finding himself a place to live. Although a few luxury villas had sprung up along the coast, he had preferred a more rural location and had opted to search the villages tucked into the foothills of the mountains for somewhere suitable. He had come across the tumbledown old farmhouse at the end of a particularly long day and had fallen instantly in love with it. With views of the mountains to the rear and a sweeping view of the sea from the front, it had been exactly what he had been searching for. He had immediately put in an offer then had to wait months while the various members of the family who owned it were contacted and persuaded to sell him their shares.

He had taken possession twelve months ago

and there was still a lot to do, but he had discovered to his surprise how much he enjoyed
working on the property. There was something
deeply satisfying about crafting and replacing
the old worn stone. It was a little like perform-
ing cosmetic surgery, he often thought; he was
taking something less than perfect and improv-
ing its appearance.

Nico parked the car and stood for a moment,
drinking in the view. The air was ripe with the
heady smell of the vines that grew in the nearby
fields and he inhaled appreciatively. There was a
good crop of grapes this year so maybe he should
think about making his own wine. It would be a
treat to sit out here next year, sipping a glass of
wine that he had produced himself. He closed
his eyes, picturing the scene: the sun turning the
sea blood red as it sank below the horizon; the
sky darkening before the first stars appeared;
the woman seated beside him, raising her glass
and smiling at him…

Nico's eyes flew open. Hurrying inside, he set

about his nightly routine—shower, change of clothes, make himself a meal—all the things he did every night when he got home. However, no matter how hard he tried, he couldn't erase that final, disturbing picture, the one of Amy seated beside him, smiling at him with such warmth in her eyes. Maybe it *was* a long time since he had seen her but it didn't feel like it, not when he could conjure up her image in the blink of an eye. However, the most worrying thing of all was that now her image was in his head, he knew that he was going to have the devil of a job getting rid of it.

CHAPTER THREE

'*EFHARISTO*. THANK YOU. That was delicious.'

Amy smiled her thanks as she and Jacob got up from the table. Breakfast had been simple but delicious: thick creamy yoghurt with honey and fresh figs followed by a selection of tiny sweet pastries. It proved that she had been right to choose this small, family-run hotel. Jacob would gain a much better idea of the Greek way of life by staying here than he would have done if they had stayed in a hotel that was part of an international chain. Hopefully, it would help him develop a better understanding of his paternal heritage.

She sighed as she followed Jacob out of the dining room. Maybe he would gain an insight into the Greek side of his heritage but unless she was prepared to tell him that Nico was his father what would it achieve? Jacob needed something solid to give him a true sense of his identity—photographs, meetings, *conversations*. At the moment his father was some shadowy figure he had never met and it wasn't enough to arm him against the taunts that had made his life such a misery lately. He needed proof that he *had* a father and the only way to give him that was by introducing him to Nico.

Amy was still worrying about it as they made their way to the beach. Although it was still early, the sun was strong so she went through the routine of applying sunscreen to Jacob as well as to herself. There was another English family staying at the hotel but the parents didn't seem concerned when their two children ran off to play before they could apply sunscreen to them. The mother shrugged when she noticed Amy watching.

'They hate having to use sun cream. I have the devil of a job putting it on them.' The woman laughed as she dropped the bottle into her beach bag. 'Mind you, I'm a bit like that myself. There doesn't seem much point coming all this way to get a tan and then coating yourself with that stuff, does there?'

Amy smiled, although she disagreed whole-heartedly with what the other woman had said. She had seen too many cases of people being badly burnt after they had failed to take adequate precautions even in England. She checked that Jacob was playing safely in the shallows with the other children then took her book out of her bag. It was the latest mystery by a favourite author but it failed to hold her attention. She kept think-ing about Nico and what she should do, whether she should tell him who Jacob was or not. It all depended on how he would react and that was something she couldn't foretell. She sighed. If it was anything like the way he had reacted when she had miscarried Jacob's twin, it would be bet-ter to keep Jacob's identity to herself.

The morning flew past. Amy spent some time helping Jacob build a sandcastle then decided it was time they got out of the sun. It was almost noon and the sun was at its peak so she opted to take him for an early lunch. Once they had put on dry T-shirts, they strolled around the headland and discovered a small *taverna* in the next bay. There was a shady terrace overlooking the beach where a couple of local fishing boats were unloading their morning's catch and she elected to sit out there, ordering a Greek salad for herself and a toasted sandwich for Jacob. They had just started to eat when Nico appeared.

Amy felt her heart leap into her throat when she saw him standing at the foot of the steps leading up to the terrace. It was obvious that he had come straight from the clinic because he was wearing a lightweight suit with an open-necked white shirt that made his olive-toned skin look more bronzed than ever. With those deep chestnut-brown eyes, that crisp black hair and those clean-cut features, he was an arresting sight and she noticed several of the women in the restaurant looking at him with interest.

Amy took a quick breath as her gaze ran over him, comparing how he looked now to how he had looked nine years ago. He was definitely thinner, she decided, thinner and even more commanding. Nico had always projected an air of confidence, of authority, of being completely in charge of himself, and it was more apparent than ever these days. He looked exactly what he was, a handsome, successful man in his prime, and the thought scared her. Once Nico found out about Jacob then she wouldn't be in control of the situation any longer. Nico would try to take charge and that was the last thing she wanted. How could she be *sure* that Nico would put Jacob's needs first? How could she *guarantee* that Jacob wouldn't get hurt?

It was that last thought which frightened her most of all, although she did have other concerns, ones which she refused to dwell on. How it would affect her to have Nico back in her life wasn't the issue.

Nico felt his breath catch when he saw Amy

sitting on the terrace. Just for a moment he was tempted to turn around and leave only that would have been far too revealing. Did he really want her to think that he had a problem about seeing her? he thought as he made himself walk up the steps. Of course not! He stopped by her table, dredging up a smile that he hoped appeared more natural than it felt.

'Hello again. I see you've discovered my favourite lunchtime haunt.'

'I had no idea that you came here,' she snapped.

'Of course not.' Nico had to stop himself taking a step back when he heard the defensive note in her voice. It was obvious that he had touched a nerve, although he wasn't sure which nerve it was. That remained to be seen. 'It's just a happy coincidence.'

He thrust that tantalising thought aside. Digging into the reason for her touchiness would be a mistake. He needed to remain detached, aloof, *distant* if he wasn't to find himself being drawn into a situation he would regret. He and Amy

Prentice had had an affair—that was the long and the short of it. He hadn't made her any promises, hadn't wanted anything more than they'd had. If Amy hadn't got pregnant then he probably wouldn't even have remembered her name...

Would he?

The question buzzed around inside his head like a pesky wasp around a jam pot but he swatted it away. He didn't intend to go down that route—it was a waste of time. Maybe he hadn't thought about her for a long time but he was very aware that somewhere in the depths of his mind, she had occupied a small space all of her own. Amy and the miscarriage had been a milestone in his life, even though he hated the idea. It implied that she had a hold over him and that was something he didn't appreciate. He preferred to live his life on his own terms and not have to account to anyone else for his actions.

'So how are you enjoying your holiday so far?' he asked, pulling out a chair. There were several empty tables he could have chosen but he was determined not to make an issue out of this encounter. The more significance he bestowed on it, the more important it would become.

'We've only been here for a day,' she shot back then flushed when she realised how rude that must have sounded. Her tone softened as she glanced at her son. 'It's been great so far, though, hasn't it, Jacob?'

'Uh-huh,' the boy mumbled, his mouth crammed full of sandwich.

Nico laughed with genuine amusement. 'I'll take that as a yes. Obviously, Jacob has worked up an appetite, so what did you get up to this morning?'

'We went to the beach for a swim and then made a sandcastle,' Amy told him, spearing a juicy black olive with her fork.

Nico looked away as she popped it into her mouth, not proof against the feelings it aroused as he watched her lips close around the ripe fruit. He took a deep breath as he picked up the menu and studied it. There was no point thinking about

Amy's beautiful mouth and the kisses they had shared. It was never going to happen again purely because he didn't intend to put himself in the position of kissing her. Not if he had any sense! As he had already discovered, Amy had the power to disrupt his life and the last thing he needed was her turning it upside down. He mustn't forget that the main reason he had moved to Constantis was for his health and he didn't need the stress.

'Dr Leonides, how lovely to see you!'

Maria Michaelis, who ran the café with her husband, Stavros, greeted him warmly as she came to take his order. Maria had been one of his first patients when he had opened the clinic. She was diabetic and had had many problems over the years, including the biggest one, her inability to get pregnant. However, after a change of medication, everything had been sorted out, although it was a little embarrassing that she now believed he was some kind of a miracle worker.

'*Kalimera*, Maria.' Nico stood up and kissed her. 'How are you today?'

'Very well, Doctor, thank you.' She patted her swollen tummy. 'This little one is certainly keeping me on my toes.'

'You mustn't do too much,' he admonished her, sitting down. He glanced at Amy, wanting to include her in the conversation as it would appear more normal that way. And keeping everything normal was vitally important, he suddenly decided. 'Maria is seven months pregnant with her first child and I keep telling her that she should rest more.'

'How wonderful! Congratulations.'

Amy smiled at the other woman and Nico felt his heart skip a beat when he realised how lovely she looked. With her light brown hair pulled back into a ponytail and her face free of make-up, she looked far too young to be the mother of the child sitting beside her. His gaze moved to Jacob and he frowned when once again he was struck by a sense of recognition. Had he met Jacob's father? Was he someone Nico had worked with in London perhaps? All of sudden he realised that he wanted to know about the man who had supplanted him in Amy's affections and fathered her child.

'Do you know if it's a boy or a girl yet? Or have you decided to wait and see when it's born?'

Amy was still talking to Maria and Nico forced himself to concentrate on the conversation. Maybe he did want answers but this wasn't the time to start asking questions. He preferred to do it when he and Amy were alone. A shiver danced down his spine at the thought of them spending time alone together but he ruthlessly suppressed it. He wasn't going down that route either!

'I wanted to wait but Stavros couldn't bear to.' Maria laughed as she patted her tummy. 'We've waited such a long time for this baby, you see, and Stavros had to know what it was. It's a boy and we're going to call him Nicolaus after the doctor because without his help we would never have had the chance to become parents. Dr Leonides did far more than we could have hoped.'

Amy smiled politely when Nico made some dismissive remark about only doing his job but she had to admit that she was surprised. Although the Nico she remembered had been an excellent doctor—thorough, committed, focused—he had never really related to his patients on a personal level. However, from what Maria had said, that was no longer the case.

The thought was intriguing. Amy had no idea what had brought about such a change in his attitude but she knew that she wanted to find out. She glanced at him, studying the strong lines of his profile as he gave Maria his order. Had something happened to make him reassess his outlook on life? He had been driven by the need to succeed when she had known him, by a desire to prove himself at the very highest levels, and yet she sensed that it was no longer the case. Nico might look much the same on the outside but inside he was a very different person, it seemed.

It was a disturbing thought when it made her see that she didn't know him as well as she had thought she did. By the time his lunch arrived, Amy had had enough of thinking about it. She and Jacob had finished eating so she asked Maria for their bill. Nico looked up and frowned.

'Please. You must allow me to pay for your lunch.'

'Oh, no, I really can't let you do that,' Amy protested, taking her purse out of her bag. 'If you can just let me know how much I owe you,' she said, glancing at Maria. Maria looked uncertainly from her to Nico, obviously unsure what to do, and Nico sighed as he put down his knife and fork.

'Let's not make an issue of it. If you prefer to pay your own bill then it's fine. I'm not going to argue with you, Amy.'

Amy flushed, realising how churlish it must have sounded to refuse his offer. She gave a little shrug as she put her purse back in her bag. 'Then thank you. It's very kind of you, isn't it, Jacob?'

Jacob nodded, although she could tell that he was growing bored and wanted to leave. Maria said something to Nico and Amy saw him frown as he glanced at Jacob and shook his head. Although Amy had no idea what Maria had said, judging by Nico's expression it was something that bothered him. All of a sudden she was struck by a need to get away. Maybe she was overreacting but there was something about the way Nico was looking at Jacob that had set all her internal alarm bells ringing. Grasping hold of Jacob's hand, she led him to the steps, pausing reluctantly when Nico called her name.

'Yes?'

'I thought you'd like to know that the girl we treated on the ferry has regained consciousness.' He shrugged but his gaze was oddly intent as it travelled from her to Jacob again.

'Oh. Right. That's good, isn't it?' Amy replied, her whole body trembling as fear overwhelmed her. Had Maria noticed the resemblance between

Nico and Jacob? she wondered sickly. Noticed it and remarked on it too?

She shot a glance at her son and felt her breath catch. Even though she had been at such pains to protect him from the sun, his skin had started to tan, making the resemblance between him and Nico all the more apparent. It didn't take a genius to see it or to realise that Jacob's chestnut-brown eyes were the mirror image of Nico's and that his nose was an exact, albeit smaller, replica of the man's. Anyone looking at them could tell they were related and all of a sudden she didn't know what to do.

Amy's heart was racing as she muttered a hasty goodbye and hurried Jacob down the steps. She could try to brazen it out, of course, deny it if Nico asked her if he was Jacob's father, but deep down she knew it would be a waste of time. Nico was already suspicious and now all she could do was try to minimise the damage it could cause. No matter what happened, she had to protect

Jacob and if that meant them leaving the island then that's what they must do.

Nico returned to the clinic after lunch although he had intended to take the rest of the day off. There were no surgeries scheduled that afternoon and he had been planning to enjoy some much-needed down time. However, meeting Amy had aroused so many questions that he knew he wouldn't rest until he found out the answers to them. He went straight to his office and closed the door, letting the silence wash over him in the hope that it would help to clear his head, but it didn't work. One question kept hammering away in his mind: was it possible that Amy's son was his child?

He sat down at his desk, struggling to make sense of the idea. It wasn't easy when he had thought that Amy had miscarried the baby they had conceived. Admittedly, it had been very early on in her pregnancy—barely six weeks, in fact—and she had refused to go to hospital afterwards, claiming that early miscarriages were extremely common and that there was nothing anyone could do. And yet as soon as Maria had asked him if Jacob was related to him, he had seen the resemblance for himself.

Closing his eyes, he pictured the boy's face, examining in his mind's eye each and every feature from the child's deep brown eyes, which were the exact same colour as his, to the shape of his nose, which was undeniably a Leonides nose. His sister, Electra, had three boys and each of his nephews had inherited the family nose. Why, they had even joked about it—he and Electra often remarking that the children could never deny their heritage with noses like that!

Nico opened his eyes and stared blankly across the room. Everything pointed towards the fact that Jacob was his son but how could he be? How could Amy have given birth to a child she had lost…unless she had lied about the miscarriage? Was that the answer? Had she deliberately misled him? Claimed that she had lost their child so she could bring it up on her own? Used it as an excuse to get *him* out of the picture? Maybe that had been her intention from the outset—she had wanted a baby but had not wanted him. He knew there were women like that, women who wanted to raise a child without any input from the father, yet he couldn't see Amy doing that. She had been too open, too honest, too *transparent* to have devised such a scheme—or so he had thought.

Anger roared through him as he realised that he really didn't know what she was capable of. He had accepted her at face value, accepted her kindness, her sweetness, her apparent lack of guile. But what if it had all been a front, a means to an end, and the end result was the child she had wanted? What if he had been nothing more than a *sperm donor* in her eyes, an unwitting one, granted, but no more than that when it came down to it? He couldn't bear to think that he had been used that way, used and then discarded, but what other conclusion could he reach when all the evidence pointed towards it being true?

Nico shot to his feet, his anger soaring as he strode to the door. Amy had a lot of explaining to do!

Amy had just finished her shower when there was a knock on the bedroom door. Jacob was lying on his bed, playing on his games console, so once she had wrapped a towel around herself, she went to answer it. It was Helena, who ran the hotel with her husband, Philo. She smiled apologetically when she saw Amy.

'*Kalispera.* I am sorry to disturb you but there is someone asking to see you.'

Amy felt a rush of fear swamp her. There was only one person who would seek her out and she wasn't sure if she was ready to face Nico yet. Not until she had worked out what she was going to say to him.

'Oh, right. Thank you.' She glanced down and shrugged, playing for time. 'I'm not really fit to see anyone right now, I'm afraid.'

'Do not worry.' Helena smiled reassuringly. 'I have shown the doctor into the sitting room and given him something to drink. There is nobody in there so you will be able to talk in private once you are dressed.'

Amy closed the door as Helena went on her way. She couldn't think of anything she wanted to do less than have a private conversation with Nico but what choice did she have? Knowing him, he wouldn't give up and go away if she failed to appear. No, he would be far more likely to come to her room and that was something she wanted to avoid. The last thing she needed was Jacob overhearing their conversation.

Gathering up her clothes, she hurriedly dressed, opting for a cotton dress in a delicate shade of green which she knew suited her. A slick of coral lipstick and a flick of mascara helped to relieve the pallor that had invaded her skin. Her hair was still wet from the shower but she didn't have time to dry it so she brushed it back from her face and secured it at the nape of her neck with a silver clip. Maybe it was silly to make such an effort with her appearance, but she needed to feel that she was in control of herself, especially as she had a feeling that she was going to need every scrap of control she could muster when she faced Nico.

'I just need to have a word with someone,' she told Jacob, slipping her feet into a pair of tan leather sandals. The heels weren't all that high but they did add an extra inch or two to her height and that would help. Nico was over six feet tall and she hated the thought of him towering over her, although at one time she had loved the way he had made her feel so small and feminine—

'I'll be in the sitting room if you want me.' Amy blanked out that thought, knowing how foolish it was. The last thing she needed at this moment was to start harking back to the past. 'I shan't be long so you're to stay here until I get back. Understand?'

'Uh-huh.' Jacob barely glanced at her, too absorbed in his game to worry about her absence.

Amy wasn't happy about leaving him on his own, however. As she made her way to the sitting room, she decided to make it clear to Nico that she had no intention of getting into a protracted discussion. Whatever he had come to say would need to be said as quickly as possible. Taking a deep breath, she pushed open the door. Nico was standing by the window and he turned when he heard her enter the room. He had his back to the light, making it impossible to discern his expression. She felt at an immediate disadvantage and decided to take the impetus from him in the hope that it might help to ease the situation.

'Helena said that you wanted to speak to me.' She gave a little shrug, as though the request didn't worry her although it did. 'I don't mean to be rude but I've left Jacob on his own, so can we keep it brief?'

'Of course.' He inclined his head although his eyes never left her face, she noticed. 'It's quite simple. I just have one question I would like you to answer: Is Jacob my son?'

CHAPTER FOUR

A DOZEN ANSWERS flew through her head but Amy knew in her heart that only one would satisfy him. What was the point of dragging this out by lying when Nico already suspected the truth? 'Yes.'

His eyes closed for the briefest of moments before he started walking towards her. Amy stepped aside, unsure what was about to happen, but he merely opened the door and left without uttering another word. Amy sank down onto a chair as all the strength drained from her limbs. Was that it? Now that Nico had his answer, was he not going to pursue the matter any further? Didn't he care that he had a son, or at least not enough to ask her any more questions?

Tears filled her eyes, tears of disappointment for Jacob, tears of disillusionment for herself.

Quite frankly, she couldn't remember feeling so let down, not even when Nico had reacted with such a sad lack of emotion when she had miscarried Jacob's twin. It made her see that any hopes she may have harboured about Nico wanting to get to know Jacob had been a waste of time. Nico wasn't interested in Jacob any more now than he had been interested in him nine years ago.

Nico sat in his car and stared across the shimmering blue expanse of the sea. He couldn't actually see it. All he could see was this greyness that seemed to have enveloped him. It felt as though it had leaked out from his very soul and consumed him.

He had a son. It should have been a time to take stock, to reassess his life and make plans for the future, but he couldn't see through the greyness. He had a son who he had known nothing about, a child who had grown up knowing nothing about him either. He didn't doubt for a moment that Amy had kept him a secret from

Jacob just as she had kept Jacob a secret from him, but why? It was a question he should have asked her, one of many that needed answering, but he couldn't face it. Not now, not when everything felt so grey and hopeless.

His hands shook as he started the engine and drove away from the hotel. It was late afternoon and the roads were busy with locals and tourists heading back to begin their preparations for the evening. Nico took his time, aware that his concentration wasn't what it should have been. It took him almost an hour to get home but it didn't matter. Nothing mattered apart from that answer Amy had given him, that tiny life-changing word: Yes.

The first stab of feeling pierced his heart and he winced. He got out of the car and watched as the sun sank below the horizon. He could see the colours now, see the gold turn to orange, see it begin to fade to a rusty red. He had no idea how long he must have stood there but there was the barest glow shimmering along the horizon when he finally roused himself. He went inside and took a bottle of water out of the fridge, gulping it down as though he had just returned from the desert. In a way, he had. He had escaped from that grey wasteland and now he needed those answers, all of them, no matter how unpalatable they might turn out to be.

Tossing the empty bottle into the bin, he went back to his car. This wasn't over, not by any means. Amy had a lot of explaining to do.

Jacob's eyelids were drooping by the time they had finished dinner. Although he put up a token resistance when Amy took him back to their room, she could tell that he was merely going through the motions. He fell asleep before she got to the end of the chapter in the book they were reading. Switching off the bedside lamp, she let herself out onto the terrace. They had a ground floor room overlooking the garden and it was peaceful out there with just the sound of the waves rolling up the beach to disturb the silence.

Sitting down on one of the wicker chairs, she let the peace wash over her, hoping it would calm her, but her nerves were too tightly strung. She didn't know when Nico would seek her out again but he would. Even if he didn't want anything to do with Jacob, he would want to make his position clear, make sure she understood exactly what she could expect from him. That was his way. He took control, made decisions, and didn't confer with anyone. However, it wasn't that simple in this instance. What Nico decided wouldn't affect only him but Jacob as well. She had come to Constantis specifically to give Jacob a link to his paternal heritage. Even though she had never expected to run into Nico, it had happened and now she needed to protect Jacob at all costs. She couldn't bear to imagine how hurt he would be if he found out who Nico was and then learned that his father had rejected him.

Quite frankly it was a risk she wasn't prepared to take so they would leave Constantis first thing in the morning. Jacob was bound to want to know why they were leaving, especially when she had made such a big deal of them staying there, but she would think up some sort of an excuse, maybe tell him they were going island hopping like the pirates of old had done. He loved stories about pirates and with a bit of luck it would convince him that there was nothing strange about the sudden change to their plans.

'We need to talk.'

Amy jumped when a figure materialised out of the darkness. She had been so lost in her thoughts that she hadn't heard Nico approaching. She pressed her hand to her throat to still the rapid pounding of her pulse. She needed to stay calm if she hoped to deal with this situation as she had to do.

'Do we?'

'Yes.' Nico stepped onto the terrace, pausing briefly to glance into the bedroom. 'I take it that Jacob is asleep.'

His tone gave nothing away and Amy bit her lip. He didn't sound angry or upset and it was hard to know how to respond. She took a quick breath, trying to match her tone to his, not an easy thing to do when she could feel the fear tumbling around inside her.

'He fell asleep before we'd finished reading his book. He was worn out from playing on the beach, I expect.'

'I expect so.' He sat down beside her. 'That and the heat. It makes a difference when you're not used to it.'

'It does. This is the first time Jacob's been away. Oh, we've had a couple of holidays in the UK but we've not been abroad before, so it's a whole new experience for him.'

'But he's enjoying it?'

'Oh, yes.' She gave a little shrug, struggling to contain her impatience. Why were they discussing the merits of this holiday when they had so many more pressing matters to worry about?

'Good. Constantis is a very beautiful place, although I doubt that was the reason you chose it for your holiday, was it, Amy?' His tone had hardened and Amy realised that the small talk was over. It was time to get down to the nitty-gritty, the real reason why Nico had come to see her.

'No. I came here because of you, Nico,' she told him bluntly.

'Really?' His brows rose. 'I thought you said that you had no idea I was living here?'

'I hadn't. I was as shocked as you were when we met on the ferry.'

'I see. So if you didn't come here to see me, then why did you come?'

'Jacob has been going through a tough time recently. He's been bullied at school because he doesn't have any contact with his father.' She shrugged. 'You never really spoke about your family, Nico, but you did mention the holidays you enjoyed here with your grandparents. I thought it might give Jacob something to relate to if we came here and he got an idea of the lifestyle, but I'm beginning to see that I made a mistake.'

'Is that a fact?'

Once again his tone gave nothing away but Amy refused to worry about it. Now that she had come this far, she intended to finish what she wanted to say.

'Yes. Jacob needs more than just a taste of the Greek way of life. He needs a real sense of his identity, solid facts about his father and his paternal heritage, and it's obvious that you aren't prepared to provide him with any of those things. That's why I've decided that we should leave Constantis. Better that than run the risk of Jacob finding out that his father doesn't give a damn about him!'

She laid it all out for him—Bang! Bang! Bang!—unconcerned as to how it made him feel. She didn't care about the effect it had had on him to discover he was a father, Nico thought bitterly, but then she had never really cared about him, had she? If Amy had felt anything for him then she wouldn't have lied about the miscarriage to get rid of him. Anger licked along his veins as he rounded on her.

'So that's it, is it? You pack your bags and leave without asking me what I want?' He laughed harshly. 'I don't know what to say, to be frank. I'm not sure if I'm more stunned by your arrogance or your stupidity!'

'There's nothing stupid about it.' She turned to him, her eyes blazing with an anger equal to his. 'You made your position perfectly clear nine years ago. You didn't want a child then or, rather, you didn't want *our* child, and it's obvious that you haven't changed your mind. What's the point of dragging this out, Nico? The sooner Jacob and I leave here, the sooner you can forget all about us. Is that really so difficult to understand?'

'Yes! It is!'

Nico could feel the emotions bubbling up inside him. It was as though the stopper had shot out of the bottle where he had kept them confined for all these years and they were suddenly free: anger and excitement, hope and fear all mingled into one huge surge of feeling that threatened to drown him. He struggled back to the surface, trying to clear his head enough so he could think, but all these feelings were getting in the way. Turning, he gripped tight hold of Amy's hands, needing something to hold on to so he wouldn't get swept away.

'Nine years ago you told me that you'd had a miscarriage and now I discover that you lied to me and that you didn't lose the child as you claimed you had. Do you have any idea how that makes me feel? Do you care?' He laughed harshly. 'I doubt it if you were prepared to go to such lengths to get what you wanted!'

'What lengths?' she demanded, trying to pull away, but he held her fast. 'I don't know what you mean.'

'Oh, come on! Of course you do. You wanted a baby, didn't you, Amy, and it just so happened that I was on the scene so you decided that I could be its father.' He shook his head. 'I'm not sure if I admire your single-mindedness or what, but you used me to get pregnant, didn't you? And then, once you'd achieved your objective, you told me that you had lost the baby. It was all very clever, really. You got exactly what you wanted and you *didn't* have to put up with the inconvenience of me cluttering up your life!'

Amy stared at him in horror. Surely he didn't believe that she was capable of such deceit? She opened her mouth to disabuse him of the idea but nothing came out, not a single word in her defence, and Nico obviously took it as proof that he was right.

'I've heard about women like you, although I've always found it hard to believe that anyone could be so cold and calculating. However, it appears that it can and does happen. Some women are prepared to go to any lengths to get what they want.

She had to say something, had to make him understand that he was wrong. She hadn't planned any of it, neither her pregnancy nor the miscarriage, or the fact that Jacob had been a twin.

'No, you're wrong, Nico. Completely and utterly wrong. I didn't…'

'Save it.' Standing up, he glared down at her and she trembled when she saw the contempt in his eyes. 'We shall leave it to our lawyers to sort this out.'

'Lawyers,' she echoed numbly.

'*Ne.* This is far too complex an issue to resolve ourselves, especially when I can't trust you to do what's right. I shall contact my lawyer in the morning. I expect he will be in touch with you very shortly.'

With that, he spun round, making it clear that he had said all he intended to say. Amy shot to her feet, knowing that she couldn't let him leave like this. She had to make him understand what had really happened before the situation deteriorated any further. She ran after him, catching hold of his jacket sleeve as he was about to step down from the terrace.

'Wait! You can't just leave like this, Nico. We can sort this out without getting anyone else involved. Once I've explained what really happened then I'm sure you'll feel very differently.'

'Really?' He turned to look at her, his eyes filled with a derision that cut her to the quick. 'You're going to make up some sort of a sob story to explain why you used me, are you?' He gave a soft little laugh that made the hair on the back of her neck stand on end when she heard the threat it held. 'Come along then, Amy, let's hear it. It should be entertaining if nothing else.'

'There's no point me telling you the truth if you refuse to believe me.' She let go of his sleeve and stepped back. 'Contact your lawyer if it's what you want to do, Nico. Maybe *he* will be prepared to listen to what I have to say, listen and believe it too!'

She went to walk away but this time it was Nico who stopped her. His hand fastened around her bare arm, his strong fingers holding her fast.

'I doubt it. I doubt if anyone will believe a word you say after I've explained how you lied and deceived me.' He hauled her to him, holding her so close that she could feel the heat from his body seeping into hers and shuddered. 'Oh, you're a highly accomplished liar—I'll give you that. I thought you were so sweet and caring but I was wrong, wasn't I? You were playing a part, that's all. You pretended to care about me and you put on a good show, good enough to fool me, and I'm not easily taken in, believe me. However, the truth is that you couldn't have given a damn about me.'

He skimmed his knuckles down her cheek in a gesture that was an insult rather than a caress. 'You were willing to trade sex for what you really wanted—a baby. And you achieved your objective, didn't you?' He laughed softly and the disgust in his voice made her cringe even though she knew it wasn't justified. 'You certainly fooled me. I actually thought it meant something when we made love but it was just a means to an end. It makes me wonder what else you're prepared to do to get what you want. It could be interesting to find out.'

Amy wasn't prepared when he bent and claimed her mouth in a searing kiss. His lips were hard, unyielding, seeking to punish more than anything else. Tears sprang to her eyes because this wasn't what she wanted. She didn't want Nico to hate her, to blame her, to feel this bitterness towards her. Maybe she should have contacted him after she had discovered that she was still pregnant but she had honestly thought she was doing the right thing. Nico hadn't wanted a child. He hadn't wanted *her*. And punishing her this way wasn't fair.

She turned her face so that his mouth slid from hers and came to rest on her cheek. She could feel the anger in his lips, feel their harshness against her skin, and her heart ached. It was obvious that he was deeply hurt as well as furiously angry and it was her fault for not making him understand what had really happened.

'I never tried to trick you, Nico.' Her voice held a desperation that made him go still. Amy knew that she had just seconds before he pushed her away and hurried on, the words spilling from her in a frantic rush. 'I never planned on getting pregnant—it just happened. And I truly thought I had lost the baby when I had that miscarriage only it turned out that I'd been expecting twins.'

Her voice broke as she tipped back her head and looked into his eyes. Even after all this time it was painful to think about the child she had lost. 'I lost one of the babies, Jacob's brother or sister, but I didn't lose him.'

CHAPTER FIVE

THE SOFT SWISH of the waves rolling up the beach was the only sound to disturb the silence. Nico could hear them rushing ashore but it felt as though he was a million miles away. It was as though he had been cut adrift, deprived of everything that was familiar. Amy hadn't lied or tried to deceive him. She had carried his child, the twin to the one she had lost, and had given birth to him. On a scale of earth-shattering events that had occurred in his life recently this had to register as a big fat ten.

Nico took a deep breath, feeling himself tremble as reaction set in. He knew that he needed to work out what he intended to do, but it was too soon. His brain simply couldn't cope with anything else at the moment. In the space of a few hours he had discovered that he was a father and that the woman who had borne his son hadn't used him as he had believed. That was more than enough to be going on with.

'Nico?'

Her voice was low, anxious, and he tensed. Amy needed his reassurance. She wanted him to tell her that everything would be all right, but he couldn't do that. Not yet. Maybe not ever. Having a child was going to make a massive difference to his life. Although he didn't know exactly how it would change, he knew that it would. He had never wanted children but it was too late now. It was a fait accompli and now he needed to readjust his whole outlook on life. Fear rushed through him at the thought and he cleared his throat, not wanting Amy to suspect how terrified he felt.

'Obviously, we have a lot to talk about but not tonight, Amy. We both need time to think about what has happened. *Ne?*'

'You do believe me, though, Nico? Believe that

I never tried to trick you?' Her voice held an urgency that made him sigh.

'Yes, I believe you. I only wish that you had told me about Jacob before now.'

'There didn't seem any point. You made it clear after the miscarriage that you didn't want a child, Nico. When I found out that I was still pregnant it seemed wrong to force you into a situation you wouldn't welcome.'

Nico grimaced because it was no more than the truth. He wouldn't have welcomed the news, although he would have accepted responsibility, of course. He would have done what was right for Amy and their baby, but would it have been enough? he wondered suddenly. Would it have been enough for Jacob to grow up knowing that his father had maintained contact with him purely out of a sense of duty?

Nico understood only too well how that felt. His own father had never made any secret of the fact that he hadn't wanted children. Christos Leonides had only agreed because it was what

Nico's mother had wanted. Ariana Leonides had come from a very wealthy family and it had been her money which had allowed his father to set up in business. Nico had always suspected that Ariana had insisted on them having children before she would agree to marry Christos. Although Christos may have acceded to her demands so he could achieve his business ambitions, he had never cared about Nico or his sister, as he had made it clear.

What if he turned out the same as his father? Nico thought sickly. What if he found it impossible to care about Jacob? At the moment Jacob seemed to be a happy and well-adjusted child. Although Amy had told him that Jacob had been bullied at school, Nico could tell that the boy knew he was loved and that made a world of difference. He could cause untold harm if he took on the role of Jacob's father only to discover that he couldn't relate to him as a father should do. It made it even harder to know what to do. Should he get involved when he wasn't sure if it would be in the child's best interests?

Amy had no idea what Nico was thinking but it was obviously something troubling if his expression was anything to go by. She bit her lip, wishing she could think of something to say to make it easier for him. Obviously, his views on fatherhood hadn't changed but if they were to deal with this situation then they had to find some sort of a compromise. The one thing she refused to do was to upset Jacob.

'Look, Nico, I realise this must have been a shock for you,' she began then stopped when a woman stepped out onto the adjoining terrace. It was Donna Roberts, the woman Amy had spoken to at the beach that morning, and she came hurrying over when she saw them.

'Have you got any aftersun?' She glanced back at her room and grimaced. 'Only Darcey's caught the sun and she's carrying on something dreadful. She's not stopped crying all evening, not even when we were trying to have our dinner. She just keeps complaining that her shoulders hurt and she feels sick.'

'I've a bottle in the bathroom,' Amy said at once. She hurried inside and fetched it, handing it to the woman with a frown. 'How bad is she?'

'Oh, not that bad. There's just a few blisters on her shoulders but they'll soon heal.' Donna sighed. 'She's driving us all mad with her moaning. Tim couldn't stand it any longer so he's taken himself off for a drink. I just wish I could have gone with him!'

'Would you like me to take a look at her?'

Amy glanced round when Nico spoke. He came over to them and she forced herself not to flinch when his arm brushed hers. All of a sudden all she could think about was that kiss. Maybe Nico had kissed her in anger, his lips seeking to punish rather than to arouse pleasure, yet the memory seemed to have lodged itself in her mind. She couldn't help comparing it to all the other times he had kissed her. Nico's kisses had aroused her like no other man's kisses had done before or since.

'I'm Dr Leonides. I run the Ariana Leonides Clinic in the town centre,' he explained and the very calmness of his tone acted like a douse of cold water.

Amy shivered as she realised how foolishly she was behaving. It didn't matter how she had felt nine years ago. The only thing that mattered was the effect it was going to have on Jacob if he found out that Nico was his father. Could she trust Nico to put Jacob's interests first? Could she trust him to care? She needed to be sure before she decided what she should do.

'Oh. Well, I don't know.'

Amy forced her thoughts back to the present when she heard the wariness in Donna's voice. 'I can vouch for Nico. He really is a doctor.'

'It's not that.' Donna gave a little shrug. 'We didn't bother buying any travel insurance, you see. Tim said it was a waste of money and it would be better spent on something else. He'll be furious if we end up with a huge medical bill.'

'There is no need to worry,' Nico said smoothly. 'I wouldn't dream of billing you for a consultation after hours.'

'Oh, I see. Well, in that case then thank you very much. It might stop Darcey moaning if a proper doctor looks at her.'

The woman smiled in relief as she led the way into her room. Amy followed her and Nico inside, pausing in the doorway as she didn't want to add to the general clutter. The room was extremely cramped thanks to the addition of two camp beds. Nico had to pick his way over to the far side where the little girl was lying huddled up, sobbing. Amy frowned. Even from this distance, she could see how red the child's skin looked.

'Hello, Darcey,' Nico said softly, crouching down beside her. 'I'm Dr Nico and I'm going to take a look at your shoulders. Your mummy said that they are very sore.'

Darcey nodded, her blue eyes awash with tears. She was about six years old and was obviously in a great deal of discomfort. 'They hurt a lot,' she whispered miserably.

'I'm sure they do.' Nico replied gently. He carefully examined the red-raw skin, his brows drawing together when he came to a patch on the child's left shoulder which was covered with a number of large fluid filled blisters. He didn't touch them, just examined them from several different angles before he stood up. His tone was flat when he addressed the child's mother but Amy could hear the anger it held.

'Your daughter has second-degree burns to her left shoulder. I suspect she is suffering from heat stroke as well. She needs immediate treatment so I shall arrange for her to be admitted to the clinic's hospital bay.'

'Hospital!' Donna exclaimed. 'Oh, no, surely that's not necessary. I mean, it's only a bit of sun-burn—nothing serious.'

'Burns like this are serious whether they are

caused by the sun or anything else,' Nico said sternly. 'Your daughter will need to be closely monitored for the next few days.'

He turned to Amy and she felt a rush of warmth envelop her when his expression softened. Did it mean that he had forgiven her for keeping Jacob's existence a secret from him? She hoped so. Maybe it was foolish but all of a sudden she realised that she didn't want to be at odds with him.

'Can you get Darcey ready? She'll need something placed over those blisters to protect them. There will be less chance of scarring if they are allowed to heal in their own time.'

'Of course,' Amy replied, rapidly running through the contents of her first aid box. She had brought it with her out of habit, not wanting to be unprepared if Jacob tripped over and cut his knee or something similar. She nodded when she remembered that she had added a pack of lint-free dressings to its contents. 'I've some dressings in my room which should be ideal.'

'Good.' Nico nodded his approval then turned

to the child's mother again. 'I shall drive you to the clinic. I suggest you contact your husband and let him know what's happened.'

'I…erm… Yes. Of course.' Donna didn't look happy as she picked up her mobile phone and went outside to call her husband.

Amy returned to her room, found the first aid box and took it back with her. Nico was speaking on his phone, making arrangements to have Darcey admitted to the hospital. Amy left him to deal with it and concentrated on making the little girl comfortable. Darcey's brother, Harvey, watched her, obviously enjoying the drama, especially as he wasn't the one who was suffering. He grinned when Amy finished.

'Darcey won't be able to go swimming now, will she?' he said gleefully.

'No.' Amy patted the little girl's hand when she started to cry. 'There'll be lots of other times when you can go swimming, sweetheart.'

'But not on this holiday,' her brother persisted.

His smile widened when Darcey let out another wail. 'Cry baby! Cry baby!'

'That is enough. It's unkind to make your sister cry like that, young man. Stop it right now.'

Nico came over to them, looking very stern as he stared at the boy in distaste. Amy hid her smile when she saw Harvey flush. She had a feeling that he didn't get reprimanded very often and couldn't help thinking that it would do him the world of good. It was her firm belief that children needed to be told when their behaviour was unacceptable and obviously Nico felt the same.

For some reason the thought filled her with a fresh sense of hope. Maybe it was wrong to see it as a sign that she and Nico could reach an agreement when they had so much to discuss, but it seemed like a good omen. She carried on getting Darcey ready, wrapping her in a sheet when the child started to shiver as the effects of her sunstroke set in. There was still no sign of her mother and she could tell that Nico was growing impatient at the delay.

'I'll go and see where Donna is,' she offered, moving to the French doors.

'*Efharisto.*' Nico glanced at the child and his mouth tightened. 'I would like to get her to the clinic as soon as possible.'

Amy nodded. The sooner Darcey started receiving treatment, the better. She went outside and found Donna standing at the end of the terrace. It was obvious that she had been crying and Amy sighed. She could do without another drama tonight, thank you very much.

'Tim's blazing,' Donna announced when Amy went over to her. 'He seems to think it's all my fault, but why should it be down to me all the time? They're his kids too and it's about time he started taking an interest in them. Most weeks he hardly sees them and when he does, he does nothing but shout at them. I tell you, it'd be easier if I was a single parent. At least I'd get some sympathy then for what I have to put up with!'

'I'm sure it's the shock that's made him so angry,' Amy replied, although she doubted it.

However, it wasn't the time to have a discussion about the man's parenting abilities. Her heart gave a little jolt as she was immediately reminded of her own concerns about Nico's abilities as a father. Could he adapt to the role? Did he even want to? She forced the questions from her mind. They were too disturbing and she would deal with them later.

'Dr Leonides is keen to leave. Have you arranged to meet your husband at the clinic or is he coming back here to look after your son?'

'He's going to meet us there.' Donna shrugged. 'After he's finished his drink, naturally.'

Amy didn't say anything. It wasn't her place to comment on the father's behaviour. She checked on Jacob, who was fast asleep, then went next door. Nico had picked Darcey up and was ready to carry her out to his car and for some reason the sight of him standing there with the child in his arms brought a lump to her throat.

She had missed all of this, missed the interaction between him and Jacob, missed seeing him holding their son in his arms when Jacob had been a baby. There was no guarantee that it would have happened, of course; who knew how Nico would have reacted when Jacob was born? However, the thought that she *and* Nico had been denied those precious memories because of her refusal to contact him not only hurt but made her feel guilty too. She had a lot of making up to do. If Nico would let her.

'We'll be off then.' Nico paused beside her and his gaze was intent as he stared down at her. Amy hastily tried to put aside those disturbing thoughts, afraid that he would read her mind. She must never forget that it was Jacob's happiness that was the most important issue. Even if she did feel guilty about what she had done, she couldn't afford to let it affect her judgement.

'Darcey's father is going straight to the clinic,' she informed him, praying that her tone of voice gave nothing away. 'He will meet you there.'

'Good. At least we won't have to wait for him to return.' He paused before he continued flatly.

'Promise me that you won't do anything hasty, Amy. We need to talk about what's happened and I don't want you leaving Constantis, if that's what you were planning to do.'

'If you're sure it's what you want, Nico,' she said softly, searching his face.

'It is.'

There was a moment when she thought he was going to say something else but in the end he swung round and left. Amy watched him carry the little girl to his car then turned away, her heart thumping heavily inside her as she went back to her own room. Jacob was fast asleep, mercifully oblivious to what had happened that night. Amy smoothed back his hair, feeling love well up inside her. She loved him so much and wanted only what was best for him but how could she be sure that involving Nico in his life would be in his best interests? She had promised Nico that they would stay on the island but there was an awful lot that needed sorting out before she reached any decisions.

She bit her lip as a wave of fear washed over

her. She would never forgive herself if she did something that, ultimately, might hurt Jacob.

Nico arrived at the clinic earlier than usual the following morning. He went straight to the hospital unit, wanting to check on Darcey Roberts before he did anything else. Although the child's injuries weren't life-threatening, he felt a strange kind of connection to the little girl. He *cared* what happened to her, cared that her parents appeared to take such little interest in her welfare. No child should be treated so indifferently. Every child should be loved and cherished, just as he wanted to love and cherish Jacob.

The thought brought him up short. Nico stood stock still as he tried to make sense of it. How could he care about the boy when twenty-four hours ago he hadn't even known Jacob had existed? The logical part of his brain rejected the idea but another part insisted it was true. He cared about Jacob. And he cared about Amy too.

Nico's heart was hammering as he entered the hospital. He had no idea what was going on but all these unfamiliar feelings scared the life out of him. It was an effort to dredge up a smile when Sophia came to greet him.

'*Kalimera*, Sophia.'

'*Kalimera*, Dr Leonides. I expect you have come to check on our new little patient.'

'*Ne*. How is she this morning?' Nico's voice sounded strained and he cleared his throat. He needed to get himself back on track rather than carry on behaving so out of character. 'Have her parents arrived yet?' he continued more firmly, glancing around the sunlit room.

He had thought long and hard when he had been planning the hospital unit, wanting to make it a pleasant place to stay as well as to provide his patients with the privacy they needed. If there were both male and female patients in the unit then a partition could be slid into place to divide the room into two separate sections. Although it wasn't possible to provide individual rooms—there simply wasn't enough space—each bed was set in its own bay. It allowed a degree of privacy that people appreciated.

'No.' Sophia's mouth thinned as she led the way to the end bay. 'They left shortly after you did last night and they haven't returned yet.'

'I see.' Nico was hard-pressed to hide his anger but there was no way that he wanted to upset Darcey. He smiled at her. 'So how do you feel this morning, little one? A bit better than you did last night, I hope.'

'My shoulders are still sore but my head doesn't hurt,' she told him solemnly. She peered hopefully past him. 'Have you brought my mummy to see me?'

'No. But I'm sure she will be here very soon,' Nico told her, gently smoothing back her hair. Darcey didn't say anything, leaving him with the distinct impression that she didn't believe him. Maybe her mother made a habit of not turning up, he thought grimly as he examined her. If that were the case then he would make it clear to her parents that it was unacceptable while the child was in his care.

He told Sophia to carry on with the treatment.

Darcey's temperature would be monitored and the area that had been burned would be kept scrupulously clean but he didn't plan to do anything else. Second degree burns—where the skin was damaged enough to cause blisters to form— usually healed on their own. Although the epidermis had been burnt, the dermis—the deeper layer of the skin—should heal without scarring. Darcey had been very lucky in many respects because the area of damage was relatively small. If it had been more extensive, it could have required plastic surgery to repair it.

'I shall come back later,' he told Sophia. 'Let me know when the parents arrive, would you? I would like a word with them.'

'Of course, Dr Leonides.' Sophia took a quick breath then hurried on. 'I'm afraid I have some news that may upset you. I shall be leaving at the end of this month. I am getting married, you see.'

'Ah. Congratulations. I am delighted for you, Sophia, although I am very sorry that you are leaving us. I had hoped to make your position here a permanent one.'

'I would have loved that, but my fiancé has been offered a job in Boston.' She sighed. 'That is the reason why we parted. I wasn't sure if I wanted to move to America to live.'

'It must have been a big decision for you but I'm sure it's the right one,' Nico said quietly.

He repeated his congratulations then went to his office, wanting to make a start on the ever-present paperwork. Although he had staff who dealt with the complexities of the Greek health service, there was always something that needed his attention. He made a note on Darcey Roberts's file to the effect that no bills should be raised. He had promised her mother that there would be no charge for her treatment and he always kept his word…

If he promised Amy that he would play a role in Jacob's life then he would have to keep his word about that too.

CHAPTER SIX

THE THOUGHT SENT alarm scudding through him. Nico got up, unable to sit calmly at his desk while his mind was in such turmoil. Walking to the window, he stared across the bay. It was too early yet for the ferries to be running but there were several fishing boats bobbing up and down on the water. Usually, he found the sight of them soothing but not that day. His head was too full of what had happened in the past twenty-four hours.

It had been the same last night—he had found it impossible to sleep when his head had been filled with so many thoughts, so many unfamiliar emotions. Discovering that he had a child had affected him in ways he was only just beginning to grasp. However, it wasn't just the thought of Jacob that had kept him awake; it was Amy as well. How did he feel about her? Because if he agreed to play a role in Jacob's life then Amy would be part of the deal too.

Nico closed his eyes, hoping that he would get a clearer idea of how he felt if he blocked out everything else. Seeing Amy again had been a shock and there was no denying it. Although he hadn't thought about her in a long time, he had quickly realised that he hadn't forgotten her. She had been tucked away in his mind and seeing her again had unleashed a lot of memories. His head began to spin as he found himself suddenly beset by some of them: long walks in the park, holding hands; pizzas eaten in front of the television while watching one of her favourite soap operas; passion-filled nights which they had spent making love…

His eyes flew open because he didn't dare go any further down that route. Not when he felt so confused. Making love with Amy had always been an emotional experience even though he had done his best to hold back. He had never had that problem with other women; in fact someone had accused him once of being so emotionally disconnected that it had felt like making love with a stranger. However, it had been very different with Amy. Right from the beginning she had made him feel things he had never felt before, engaged him both mentally as well as physically. Amy had touched him in ways he would never have believed possible and the thought alarmed him.

Nico gazed at the fishing boats without actually seeing them. If he agreed to be Jacob's father then how could he be sure that he wouldn't fall under Amy's spell once more? Oh, he could tell himself that he was strong enough to resist, but was he? Really? Recalling that kiss they had shared last night, he couldn't put his hand on his heart and swear that he was immune to her. Maybe he had kissed her in anger but there had been a moment just before she had turned away when anger had been replaced by another emotion equally strong, and it was that which worried him.

How could he get involved with her and Jacob when the future was so uncertain? Although he had made a full recovery following his heart attack, his doctor had warned him that it could happen again. Although he hoped to live a long and full life, he couldn't guarantee it, which meant he had to consider the impact it could have on other people. That hadn't been an issue before; however, the situation had changed. To put it bluntly, what good would it do Jacob and Amy if he fostered a relationship with them only to have it cut short?

Amy was surprised to see the Roberts family in the dining room when she and Jacob went in for breakfast. Donna Roberts waved as they sat down and Amy waved back, although she couldn't help wondering what they were doing there. If Jacob had been rushed off to hospital then nothing would have induced her to leave his side. Donna came over as Amy was pouring herself a cup of coffee.

'I just wanted to say thanks for last night. At least we didn't have to put up with Darcey's moaning all night long!'

'Oh, right.' Amy summoned a smile although it was hard to believe that anyone could be so heartless. 'You decided not to stay at the hospital with her then?'

''Course not! She's perfectly safe there and to tell you the truth I was glad to get a break from her.' Donna laughed. 'There's nothing gets you down more than a kid who won't stop whining, is there?'

Amy didn't say anything as Donna returned to her table. The family had finished their breakfast and, from the look of it, they were ready to head off to the beach. It was hard to believe that they were going to spend the day enjoying themselves instead of rushing off to be with their daughter.

She and Jacob finished their breakfast and went to the beach as well but Amy found it difficult to settle. The memory of what had happened the previous night preyed heavily on her mind. Should she have promised Nico that they wouldn't leave the island? At the time, she had felt that she'd had no choice, not when he had been so anxious to get Darcey to the clinic, but had it been the right thing to do? She had no idea how he truly felt about Jacob and that was the most worrying thought of all. There was no way on earth that she would she risk Jacob getting hurt. She intended to protect him at all costs, as any parent should protect their child.

The thought naturally reminded Amy about poor little Darcey, all on her own in the clinic. She couldn't bear to imagine the little girl's distress when her parents failed to turn up and decided that she had to say something. She got up and went over to where Donna and her husband were sunbathing.

'I was just wondering when you were going to visit Darcey,' she explained when Donna looked up.

'Oh, sometime this evening, I expect.' Donna yawned. 'There's no point wasting the day sitting around in the hospital, is there?'

'Won't she miss you, though?' Amy persisted.

'Maybe.' Donna shrugged. 'But you can't spend your whole life running round after your kids. You need a bit of time to yourself.'

Donna closed her eyes, making it clear that the subject was closed. Amy went back to her towel and lay down but she still couldn't relax. It was as though her thoughts were on a merry-go-round—she kept thinking about that promise she had made to Nico and the possible repercussions from it. In the end she couldn't stand it any longer so when Jacob came back to get a drink she told him that they were going into town, using the excuse that they would pop into the clinic to see Darcey. Hopefully, she might get a chance to speak to Nico while they were there too. Quite frankly, anything had to be better than sitting here, wondering what was going to happen!

Jacob grumbled a bit about having to leave

the beach but he soon cheered up when he discovered they were going to use the local bus. It meandered its way to the town centre, stopping at several villages en route to pick up more passengers so that it was packed when it finally arrived. Amy helped Jacob alight then looked around, wishing she had asked Helena for directions to the clinic. There were a number of roads leading off from the main square and she had no idea which way to go. They could be wandering around for ages, trying to find the place.

'Look, Mum. Over there. It's a fort!'

The excitement in Jacob's voice brought her mind back to the fact that this holiday was supposed to be for his benefit. Maybe she did need to speak to Nico, but not at the expense of ruining Jacob's day. She smiled at him.

'Want to go and take a look?' she suggested, laughing when he bounced up and down with excitement.

'Yes!'

He went haring off, leaving Amy to follow at

a more sedate pace. It was market day and there were a number of stalls set up around the square. She decided to take a look at what they were selling after they had visited the fort and treat them to a few souvenirs to remind them of Jacob's first holiday abroad. She grimaced. Bearing in mind what had happened since they had bumped into Nico on that ferry, she was unlikely to forget it!

Nico saw his final patient out then checked with Theodora, their receptionist, that there were no last-minute appointments. Morning surgery had been unusually quiet which meant he had finished early for once. He decided to make the most of the time and go into town. With all that had happened recently, he hadn't given any thought to the contents of his fridge and he was fast running out of fresh food. Maybe he should think about inviting Amy and Jacob for dinner one night, he mused as he set off and then just as hurriedly dismissed the idea. Until he and Amy talked everything through and decided what they intended to do, he shouldn't get too involved.

The thought weighed heavily on him as he walked into the town centre. He knew what he wanted to do but he wasn't convinced it was right. Leaving aside the matter of his health, what if his initial enthusiasm waned? He had never had very much to do with children other than during the course of his work. Although he was fond of his sister's boys, he certainly hadn't yearned for a child of his own, never felt that he was missing out by not having a family. It wasn't difficult to imagine the damage it could cause if he formed a relationship with Jacob only to discover that it wasn't what he wanted and disappeared from the child's life at a later stage. The last thing he wanted was for Jacob to grow up thinking that his father hadn't wanted him. He knew from bitter experience how that felt.

Nico made his way to the main square where the weekly market was being held and bought a selection of fruit and vegetables as well as some *horiatiko psomi*—a type of bread that was baked outdoors in wood-burning stoves. He knew most of the stallholders and exchanged pleasantries with them, thinking as he did so how different his life was these days. When he had lived in California he'd had a housekeeper to make sure his every need was catered for. Although he had taken it for granted at the time, it struck him now what an unreal existence it had been. He much preferred this hands-on approach. It kept him grounded, made him see what really mattered, which wasn't success and making money as he had believed once. How surprised Amy would be if he told her that.

As though thinking about her had conjured her up, she suddenly appeared. She had Jacob with her and they were standing beside a stall that sold baklava—the delicious, honey-soaked pastries that were so popular all over Greece. Nico felt his heart start to pound as he came to a sudden halt. They were too interested in selecting their pastries to have noticed him so all he needed to do was make his way through the stalls and he would be able to avoid them. It was the sensible thing to do bearing in mind that he still had no real idea what he should do about Jacob, so why did he feel this knot of excitement building inside him? Why did he suddenly want to be with them more than he had wanted anything before?

Nico couldn't explain it. All he knew was that his heart was telling him to go over to them even though he knew it could be a mistake. And for a man like him, who had always known his own mind, it came as a shock to find himself so ambivalent. What hope did he have of reaching any major decisions about the future when he couldn't even make up his mind about this?

'Try some of those. The ones with the pistachio nuts on them. They're my favourite.'

Amy swung round, a silent *Oh!* forming on her lips when she saw Nico standing behind her. Maybe she had been planning to go to the clinic but she hadn't expected to see him here in the market and it threw her completely off balance. Heat rushed up her face as she hurriedly turned back to the pastries.

'They all look so delicious, it's hard to choose,' she murmured, not wanting to think about the reasons why her heart was racing. It was only natural that she should feel keyed up when she still needed to find out what he planned to do about Jacob, she told herself, but deep down she knew it was only partly true. Being near Nico affected her and there was no point trying to pretend that she was indifferent to him. She took a deep breath and used it to shore up her emotions. At the end of the day, this was all about Jacob; it wasn't about her and Nico.

The stallholder popped the pastries into a box. She obviously knew Nico and chatted away to him as she fastened the box with a length of pale pink ribbon. She handed it to Amy, shaking her head when Amy tried to pay her.

'They are a gift,' Nico said quietly beside her.

'Kara and her husband are patients of mine and it's her way of thanking me.'

'Oh, but I couldn't possibly accept them without paying for them,' Amy protested, taking out her purse.

'Kara will consider it an insult if you refuse.' Nico caught hold of her hand. 'Just thank her and she will be more than happy, believe me.'

'I…ehem…*efharisto*,' Amy murmured, holding herself rigid when she felt the tremor that was working its way up her arm. She quickly withdrew her hand, determined that she wasn't going to let Nico think that his touch still had the power to affect her. The days when Nico could turn her insides to jelly with the lightest of touches were long gone. 'Thank you very much. I'm sure we shall enjoy them.'

The woman nodded graciously then said something to Nico and even though Amy couldn't understand a word, she knew it was about Jacob. Had Kara spotted the resemblance between him and Jacob? she wondered, glancing at him. She sighed because it was obvious from his expression that she was right. People only had to see him and Jacob together to know they were related. Now all she could do was pray that nobody would say anything to Jacob.

The thought made her feel sick with worry. As they moved away from the stall, Amy realised that she needed to avoid it happening again until she knew exactly what Nico intended to do. Taking hold of Jacob's hand, she led him towards the bus stop. Although she felt bad about not visiting Darcey, she couldn't take the risk of going to the clinic and having other people remark on the resemblance between them. Jacob would be devastated if he found out that Nico was his father only to learn that Nico didn't want anything to do with him.

'We'd better make our way back to the hotel,' she said, adopting her most upbeat tone. The thought of Jacob's hurt and bewilderment if he suffered such a rejection was more than she could bear. She smiled as she held up the box of

pastries, not wanting Jacob to suspect that anything was wrong. 'Thank you for these, although
by rights they belong to you. Are you sure you
don't want them, Nico?'

'Certainly not.' He laughed, his handsome face
lighting up with sudden amusement. 'I shall be
as fat as pig if I eat them all myself.'

Amy grimaced. 'Hmm, maybe I should give
them a miss too. I'm not sure if my waistline can
cope with all those zillions of calories.'

'Oh, I don't think you need worry about that.
Your figure is perfect, if you want my opinion.'

Amy felt heat invade every cell in her body
as his eyes swept over her. That he liked what
he saw wasn't in doubt. Although she'd had her
share of admirers over the past few years, she
had avoided getting involved in another relationship. It hadn't been difficult. Jacob came first and
there was no way that she would risk upsetting
him by bringing a stranger into their lives, plus
she had never met anyone who she had wanted
to spend her life with…

Except Nico.

Pain pierced her heart and she turned away. She had loved him so much but she had learned the hard way that love wasn't always reciprocated. Nico hadn't loved her. He couldn't have done if he had been so relieved when she had seemingly lost their child. The thought was almost too painful to bear but she had to see the situation for what it was. Even if Nico did agree to play a role in Jacob's life, he wouldn't be interested in playing a role in hers.

'Would you like to come to my house for dinner one evening?'

'I beg your pardon?' Amy stopped when Nico spoke, wondering if she had misheard him.

'You and Jacob. Would you like to come to my house for dinner one evening?' Nico's expression softened as he glanced at Jacob who had wandered off to look at a stall selling hand-carved wooden toys. 'It would be an ideal opportunity for us to get to know one another better.'

'Does that mean you've decided what you intend to do?' Amy asked, holding her breath.

'I suppose it does.' He shrugged and she could tell by the bemused expression on his face that it was as big a shock to him as it was to her.

'You need to be sure, Nico. Once we tell Jacob who you are, you can't change your mind. You do understand that?'

'Yes. Which is why I am not proposing that we tell him just yet.' He took a deep breath and his expression was sombre all of a sudden. 'There are things I need to tell you first, Amy, and they could influence how you feel about my involvement in Jacob's life.'

'What things?' she demanded. 'What are you talking about, Nico?'

'We can't discuss it here. We need to speak in private.' He glanced round when the rumble of an engine announced that their bus had arrived. 'How would tomorrow evening suit you? Do you have plans or can you come then? I can pick you up after clinic closes. Around five p.m. if that's convenient.'

'That's fine,' she murmured, her head spinning. What on earth did Nico have to tell her that was so important it could affect how she felt about them telling Jacob that he was his father? As they boarded the bus, Amy tried to make sense of it but it was impossible. She would have to wait until the following evening to find out what Nico meant and the thought of having to wait all that time wasn't easy. She had a horrible feeling that she wasn't going to like what Nico told her.

CHAPTER SEVEN

BY THE TIME surgery ended the following day, Nico was having serious doubts about what he had done. Inviting Amy and Jacob to dinner had seemed like a good idea at the time. After all, he needed her to know exactly what it could mean if he became involved in Jacob's life and subsequently suffered another heart attack. However, he had to admit that he wasn't looking forward to telling her. Admitting that he was vulnerable in any way didn't come easily to him, and it was especially hard when it was Amy who would be hearing his confession. Although he knew it was stupid, he hated to think that she might view him as less than the man he had been afterwards.

He tried to shrug off the thought as he drove to her hotel. It was a little after five when he arrived and Amy and Jacob were sitting on the terrace, waiting for him. Nico took a deep breath before he opened the car door. Maybe his ego was about to suffer a major blow but there was no way that he could avoid telling Amy the truth.

'All ready?' he asked, walking over to them.

His gaze skimmed over her, taking stock of the coral-pink dress she had chosen to wear. Although it wasn't an expensive designer number like the women he had known in California would have worn, it suited her, he decided, the colour setting off her soft brown hair and adding a glow to her lightly tanned skin. She looked so young and so lovely as she stood there holding Jacob's hand that he was overwhelmed by a sudden need to touch her. Bending, he kissed her on the cheek, his lips lingering on her warm, sweet-smelling skin as a host of emotions flowed through him. He cared about her and there was no point pretending that he didn't. He cared about her and, what's more, he always had.

Nico drew back, trying to hide his shock as he turned to Jacob. It was hard to maintain a calm front but he didn't have a choice. He couldn't let Amy know how he felt, especially when she had no idea about his heart attack. It was bound to affect how she viewed him when she found out that he was damaged goods.

'I thought we could go down to the cove and try our hand at fishing before dinner,' he told Jacob, doing his best to ignore the pain that thought aroused. 'Have you ever been sea fishing before?'

'No.' Jacob's face lit up with excitement. 'If we catch any fish then can we cook them for dinner?'

'I don't see why not.'

Nico ruffled the boy's hair, feeling his heart swell as he was overwhelmed by an unfamiliar rush of emotion. It was an effort to stop himself scooping the child into his arms and hugging him. It was what he should have done from the day Jacob was born, he thought. He should have been there for him right from the beginning and the fact that he hadn't been was something he would always regret. If he hadn't reacted so crassly when Amy had miscarried Jacob's twin then she would have told him that she was still pregnant and he wouldn't have missed out on all that precious time.

Nico's heart was heavy as he led the way to the car. He helped Jacob into the back and fastened his seat belt then opened the passenger door for Amy. She looked up as she slid into the seat and he could tell that she had guessed how emotional he was feeling. He closed the door and went round to the driver's side without saying anything. Until she knew about his heart attack, he couldn't reveal his feelings, shouldn't by rights even have any.

He took a deep breath to batten down the pain as he started the engine. If it turned out that Amy considered he wasn't a good enough prospect to take on the role of Jacob's father then her decision had to be final.

Amy could feel her anxiety building as they drove to Nico's home. On any other occasion she would have enjoyed the journey too. The scenery was stunning, the vivid blue of the sea contrasting dramatically with the deep greens and greys of the mountains. However, she couldn't rid herself of the memory of how Nico had looked when he had ruffled Jacob's hair. It had been the sort of casual gesture anyone might have made and yet she knew that it had been a defining moment for him. She had seen it in his eyes and understood the effect it had had on him. What she didn't understand was why he had looked so sad afterwards. Whatever secret he was harbouring, it was obviously important.

The thought triggered another bout of anxiety so that she didn't realise they had arrived until she heard Jacob scramble out of the car. She got out as well and looked around in astonishment. If she had been asked to guess where Nico lived, she would have opted for somewhere far more palatial than this rustic old farmhouse. True the views were stunning but it was a world away from what she had expected.

'So, what do you think?' Nico came and stood beside her, pushing his hands into his pockets, and Amy realised in surprise that he was nervous.

'The view is stunning,' she told him truthfully, trying not to read any significance into the fact that he seemed to set any store by her opinion. She gave a little shrug. 'I suppose, if anything, I'm surprised that you chose a place like this. It's not what I expected.'

'You thought I'd opt for something flashier, a huge, luxurious, modern villa with all the bells and whistles.' He laughed wryly. 'Been there, done that, and I am not planning to do it again!'

'Really. It sounds as though you have had a massive change of heart, Nico. A luxury lifestyle was always high on your agenda before.'

'True.' He shrugged but his expression was guarded all of a sudden. 'I did have a major rethink about my life and how I intended to live it, but then a lot of people do. Things happen that make you redefine what you really want, as you must have discovered for yourself. Having a child and deciding to raise it on your own can't have been easy, Amy.'

'If that was meant as a rebuke—' she began, but he shook his head.

'It wasn't. I didn't invite you here to start an argument. I just wondered how you coped with looking after a baby. You must have had to go back to work, I imagine, so how did you manage then?'

'My parents helped. They were wonderful and looked after Jacob until he was old enough to go to nursery,' she explained quietly.

'It still can't have been easy for you,' he said flatly.

'No, it wasn't but it was worth it.' She gave a little shrug because it seemed pointless getting hung up on past events. 'That's all over and done with now and we need to decide what happens from here on. You said that you had something to tell me?'

'That's right. I do. But let's leave it until after

dinner. I promised Jacob that we would go fishing and if I'm not mistaken he intends to hold me to it too!' he added wryly as Jacob came rushing over to them.

He took Jacob inside so they could sort out their fishing tackle but Amy stayed where she was. She couldn't insist that Nico explain what the problem was right this very minute. He would tell her in his own good time and until then she would have to try not to worry too much. She grimaced. Bearing in mind that it was obviously going to have a major impact on any decisions she made, it wasn't the easiest thing to do.

They caught three fish and Jacob was ecstatic because he had caught the biggest one of all. Nico helped him to reel it in then showed him how to scrape off its scales.

'Well done!' he declared after Jacob had finished. He asked Jacob to descale the other fish while he performed the messier job of gutting them, realising to his surprise how much he enjoyed teaching the child to perform such tasks. His grandfather had taught him when he'd been roughly the same age as Jacob was and it felt remarkably good to discover a link to those happy times. Somewhere along the way he had forgotten how much he had enjoyed spending time with his grandfather; however, being with Jacob like this had reawoken a lot of wonderful memories.

Once the fish were ready, they popped them into a plastic bag and carried them back to the house. Amy had opted to sit on the terrace rather than accompany them to the beach and he had been relieved. Not only had it given him a chance to spend time alone with Jacob but it had afforded him some welcome breathing space as well.

He sighed as he and Jacob made their way back up the path. He knew that Amy was longing to hear what he had to say but he was nowhere near as eager to tell her. He kept wondering how it would affect the way she saw him even though he knew how foolish it was. However, foolish or not, he couldn't bear to think that he would be somehow diminished in her eyes. He grimaced. Even if his ego did suffer a massive dent, he still had to tell her the truth. It wouldn't be right to withhold information like that when it would influence any decisions she made about his involvement in Jacob's life.

'We caught three fish, Mum, and I caught the biggest one!' Jacob was bubbling over with excitement as he showed Amy the fish.

'Brilliant! Well done,' she declared, smiling at him. She looked up when Nico came to join them and he had to steel himself when he saw the warmth disappear from her eyes. 'He's a natural fisherman, wouldn't you say?'

'Indeed I would.'

Nico cleared his throat. There was no point wishing that Amy had looked at him with the same degree of warmth. After all, he had let her down, hadn't he? Oh, maybe he hadn't known that she was still pregnant but he hadn't made any attempt to contact her after he had left London. At the time he had honestly believed it was for the best; their relationship was over and they needed to make a clean break. However, now he couldn't help thinking that he had should have kept in touch. She had been so upset after the miscarriage and he had been less than supportive…

He drove the thought from his mind because he simply couldn't deal with it when there was so much else to think about. Taking the bag into the kitchen, he set about filleting the fish. Jacob had followed him so Nico showed him how to remove the bones from the fish, another task the boy obviously enjoyed doing.

'Excellent,' he told him. 'You've made a first rate job of that.'

Jacob looked as pleased as punch on hearing that and Nico couldn't help recalling his own childhood and how he had longed to receive a word of praise from his father. It had never happened but he made a note never to forget to praise

Jacob when he had done something well. He bit back a sigh because who knew if he would get the opportunity again. It all depended on what Amy decided once she learned about his health.

That thought kept him company as he fired up the barbeque. He showed Jacob how to rub the fish with olive oil and seasoning then placed the fillets in a metal cage and laid them on the grill. He held up his hand when Jacob eagerly stepped forward to help. 'This is really hot so you mustn't get too close. Perhaps you could help your mum make a salad? Everything's in the fridge plus there's some bread in that big stone jar on the dresser—we'll have that as well.'

Jacob happily led Amy inside, chattering away about how much fun it had been to catch his own supper. Nico turned the fish over, not wanting them to burn and ruin the whole experience for his son. His heart caught because Jacob *was* his son and he always would be no matter what Amy decided to do.

It was a moment of such profundity that he had

to force himself to concentrate on what he was doing. However, he could feel the tension that had been gathering momentum all day reach a crescendo. So much depended on Amy's decision. It wasn't overstating the case to say that his whole future was in her hands.

Jacob decided to watch some cartoons on one of the television channels after they had finished dinner. The fact that the characters were speaking Greek didn't seem to faze him one bit. Amy gave him a bowl of ice cream and left him to enjoy the programme. Nico had already cleared away the dishes when she went back outside and had a pot of coffee ready as well. Her brows rose.

'My, my, you are domesticated. What happened to the guy who didn't know how to boil water let alone turn it into coffee?'

'He had a rude awakening when he moved here.' Nico grinned but she could see the wariness in his eyes. Her heart caught because there was no doubt that whatever he wanted to tell her was going to have a major impact. 'Hiring a housekeeper to tend to my every need wouldn't have gone down well with the islanders, believe me.'

'So you do it all—the cooking, the cleaning, the shopping?' Amy knew that she was talking for the sake of it. While they were discussing such mundane matters, she could put off the moment when he would tell her his secret.

'Mmm. I also do most of the work on the house as well.' He waved a hand around the terrace. 'This is all my own handiwork. The terrace had collapsed when I bought this place and I rebuilt it.' He gave a self-mocking laugh. 'Maybe I haven't wasted all that training I underwent to become a plastic surgeon!'

'Do you miss it?' she asked quietly, sitting down. 'Surgery, I mean.'

'Sometimes.' He shrugged. 'But I don't miss the lifestyle I had. I prefer it here. It's far more real.'

'So what happened to your desire for fame and fortune?'

'I discovered that it wasn't what I really wanted at the end of the day.' He paused and she held her breath, sensing that he was about to reveal whatever was troubling him. She steeled herself, but nothing could have prepared her for what he said.

'I had a heart attack, you see. Quite a serious one, serious enough to put me in ICU for a couple of weeks.' He looked at her and she could tell that he was trying to gauge her reaction.

Could he tell how shocked she was? she wondered sickly. How terrified she felt at the thought of him having been seriously ill, possibly dying? The pain that thought aroused was so intense that she gasped and she saw his expression darken.

'Are you all right?' He took hold of her hand and held it tightly. 'I'm sorry. I shouldn't have dropped it on you like that without any warning...'

'You're all right now, though, aren't you, Nico?' Her voice echoed with a fear she couldn't disguise and she felt him go tense.

'Yes. I've made a lot of changes to the way I

live and I'm fine.' He released her hand and stood up, walking to the end of the terrace to stare out across the bay. His voice sounded strained when he continued, as though he was struggling to contain his emotions, and her heart ached for him. Dealing with such a life-changing event couldn't have been easy.

'My doctors put it down to the fact that I had been under far too much pressure so that's why I decided I needed to reassess my life. However, it would be wrong to assume that it will never happen again, Amy. That's why you need to decide what we should do about Jacob. What happens if we tell him I'm his father and in a few years' time I have another heart attack and die?'

Amy couldn't bear it. She simply couldn't bear to hear him say such a thing. Jumping to her feet, she went and put her arms around him. His body was rigid, unyielding. Nico was holding on to his control because it wasn't his way to give in to his emotions. But if ever there was a time when he needed to drop his guard, it was now.

'Don't say that, Nico. You mustn't even think it!' She drew him closer, feeling the rigid muscles relax the tiniest bit, and it was all the encouragement she needed. Nico was hurting and she wanted to comfort him any way she could.

Reaching up, she slid her hands around his neck and drew his head down so she could kiss him. His lips were cold at first, cold and stiff, and her heart ached at the thought of the rejection she was about to suffer. Then all of a sudden she felt a rush of warmth flow from his mouth into hers, flow right through her in a hot and hungry tide that made her head spin. Now it was Nico who was kissing her and kissing her with a desire she remembered only too well. As his lips claimed hers, teasing, tasting, arousing her passion, she gasped. She had never felt this desire with anyone else, never longed for any other man's kisses the way she had longed for Nico's. She wasn't sure what it meant but it must mean something.

She was trembling when he let her go. It took every scrap of strength she could muster to walk back to her chair and sit down. Nico was still standing at the end of the terrace and the expression on his face was impossible to read. Had the kiss affected him as much as it had affected her? She couldn't tell but she knew that she mustn't make the mistake of reading too much into it. At the end of the day, she didn't want to be left with a broken heart again. And she most definitely didn't want Jacob to suffer.

The thought made her go cold. All of a sudden she could imagine the harm it could cause if Jacob grew to love Nico—as he would—and something happened to him. Would it be fair to place the child in that position? To allow Jacob to grow attached to his father when there was a chance that he might lose him? Questions whirled around inside her head, making her feel so giddy that she couldn't separate one from another let alone find any answers to them. It was a moment before she realised that Nico was speaking to her.

'I'm sorry,' she murmured, desperately trying to pull herself together, but it was impossible when she found herself suddenly beset by a whole new set of questions. How would *she* feel if something happened to Nico? Lost? Devastated? Bereft? She knew that she would feel all of those things and yet she couldn't understand why. Nico hadn't been part of her life for so long that it shouldn't matter this much if anything happened to him.

'I think it's time I took you and Jacob back to the hotel,' he repeated in a tone that revealed very little about how he was really feeling.

Amy nodded, realising that it would be for the best. She needed time to think about what she had learned, base her decision on logic rather than emotion. She shuddered because she knew just how hard it was going to be. Nico aroused far too many emotions inside her to separate them from rational thought. All she could do was hope that she could find a solution that would work for all of them: her, Nico and, most important of all, Jacob.

Amy went inside and told Jacob they were leaving. He was reluctant to abandon his cartoons but cheered up when she told him he could play on his games console when they got back to the hotel. Nico ushered them both into the car and drove them back, pulling up outside the front door. Dinner had just finished and she could hear the clatter of china coming from the dining room as Helena and Philo cleared up. Their teenaged son, Yanni, was helping them, loading glasses onto a tray to carry them down to the basement kitchen. It all appeared so normal that Amy had difficulty believing what had happened in the past hour. Nico had told her that he could die: could it be true?

'Nico,' she began then stopped when there was a loud crash followed by a blood-curdling scream from inside the hotel.

Nico leapt out of the car before she could unfasten her seat belt and raced inside. Amy went to follow him, pausing when she realised that Jacob was hard on her heels. Until she had a better idea of what had happened, it seemed wiser to keep him out of the way.

'You go and wait in here,' she told him, opening the sitting room door. 'I'll be back in a moment once I've seen what's happened.'

Jacob didn't argue, thankfully enough. He went and sat down on the sofa, looking scared. Amy bent down and gave him a hug. 'It's OK, sweetheart. Nico's a doctor so if anyone's hurt then I'm sure he can help them.'

Jacob brightened up at that. Picking up an abandoned comic left there by some previous holidaymakers, he settled down to read. Amy hurriedly made her way to the dining room, her heart sinking as she took in the scene that met her. Yanni was lying in a sea of broken glass at the bottom of the steps leading down to the kitchen. There was a huge gash down his right arm and another down the right side of his chest. Both were bleeding copiously so she grabbed some clean napkins off the shelf and hurried down the steps.

'Here. Use these.' She handed Nico several napkins then used another couple to stem the blood flowing from the teenager's arm. The cut was deep, a huge slice of flesh having been partially severed and hanging by a thread. Yanni was moaning in agony and Nico shook his head.

'He needs something for the pain. Can you stay with him while I fetch my bag from the car?'

'Of course.'

Amy carried on with what she was doing, using both hands to stem the flow of blood. Yanni was shivering violently now and she guessed that he was going into shock. He urgently needed fluids to compensate for the blood he was losing so it was a relief when Nico returned and handed her a bag of saline and everything she needed to set up a drip. Helena was standing in the corner, sobbing, while Philo was staring blankly at them. Amy beckoned him over, knowing it would help if she gave him something to do.

'Can you find something to hang this drip on?' she asked, deftly inserting the cannula into Yanni's arm. 'We need to get some fluids into him as quickly as possible.'

Philo hurried away, coming back a few minutes later with an old-fashioned coat stand. Amy had the line set up by then and she nodded her approval as she hung the bag of saline on one of the coat hooks. 'That's perfect, thank you.'

Nico had administered an injection of morphine along with an anti-emetic so Yanni wasn't in quite so much pain. However, it was obvious that he urgently needed treatment. She wasn't surprised when Nico quietly informed her that he had called an ambulance. It arrived a short time later by which time she and Nico had managed to stop the bleeding.

'I'll take him straight to Theatre,' he told her as they helped the paramedics load the boy onto a stretcher. 'I need to check that there's no muscle damage to the arm or that will cause problems for him in the future.'

'His chest is badly cut too,' Amy said, sotto

voce, although it was doubtful if Yanni could hear her now that the morphine had taken effect.

'It is. It's going to need plastic surgery if he isn't to be left with an ugly scar.'

'Well, he couldn't be in better hands,' she said, smiling at him.

'Thank you.'

Nico returned her smile. He appeared to be about to say something else but in the end he turned away. Amy frowned as she watched him help Helena into his car. What had he been going to say? Had it been something to do with his patient or had it been of a more personal nature?

A shiver danced down her spine and she hugged her arms around herself as she went back inside the hotel. She knew that she was allowing her emotions to get the better of her and it was scary to realise just how vulnerable she was. What Nico had told her tonight had been a massive shock and there was no point denying it. Maybe she hadn't seen him for a very long time, but somewhere at the back of her mind, the thought that he was living his life as he had chosen to do had lingered. In a strange way it had been a comfort. Now everything had changed and she needed to weigh up the effect it could have on Jacob if Nico died.

She took a deep breath, trying to batten down the searing pain that pierced her heart at the thought. It was Jacob's feelings which mattered. Not hers.

CHAPTER EIGHT

IT HAD BEEN a while since Nico had performed such delicate and intricate surgery but he soon found his confidence surging back as he set about the familiar routine. As he had feared there was damage to one of the major muscles in the boy's arm and he attended to that first, painstakingly piecing everything back together. Although Yanni would probably suffer some after-effects—possible weakness in the arm or a lack of co-ordination—Nico knew that his swift intervention would save the boy years of heartache and was pleased. Maybe he should think about utilising his skills to help other people in Yanni's position?

It was the first time that he had reconsidered his decision to forsake surgery and it was unsettling. He had been so sure of what he was doing but all of a sudden everything seemed to be up in the air. He forced the disturbing thoughts from his head as he concentrated on the job at hand, tidying up the flap of skin before stitching it back into place with the most exquisitely tiny stitches. Sofia, who was acting as lead theatre nurse, shook her head.

'I did not know it was possible to produce work like this, Doctor. It's amazing!'

'I'd be rather good at embroidery, don't you think?' Nico replied, smiling at her over his mask.

'Very good. I know who to ask if I need my wedding dress embroidered!'

Everyone laughed and it helped to lighten the rather tense mood. Although they were all skilled professionals, Nico knew that none of them had dealt with this type of situation before. Leonardo, the young doctor he had hired a couple of weeks earlier, seemed particularly fascinated so Nico made sure that he could see what he was doing. Maybe he should also think about passing on his skills to some of the younger doctors? he mused. After all, it seemed a shame to possess all this knowledge and not make use of it.

By the time everything was sorted it was five a.m. and he could tell that everyone was as exhausted as he was. 'Thank you all,' he said, looking around the small group who had worked so hard to support him. 'You've done a wonderful job and it's thanks to you that Yanni should regain full use of his arm eventually.'

He was deeply touched when a spontaneous round of applause broke out and had to leave Theatre in rather a rush in case he broke down. He felt incredibly emotional and put it down to being back in Theatre after such a long absence, although deep down he suspected that there was more to it than that.

He went to find Helena and Philo, who had spent the night in Reception. They leapt to their feet when he appeared and he saw the fear on their faces and understood. Now that he had a child of his own, he knew how it must feel to fear the worst.

'Yanni is fine,' he said, swallowing the lump in his throat that thought evoked. 'The operation went extremely well and although there are bound to be a few problems, I'm confident that in time your son will regain full mobility in his arm.'

Helena burst into tears and sank back down onto a chair. Philo shook his head, seemingly unable to take it all in. Nico patted him on the shoulder, an unprecedented move for him. 'Yanni will be fine, Philo. Believe me.'

Philo still couldn't get any words out and settled for vigorously pumping Nico's hand instead. Nico gave the couple a moment to collect themselves then explained that a nurse would be along shortly to take them to see Yanni. Although the boy needed peace and quiet to recover from the operation, he knew that the parents desperately needed to see him. If it were Jacob lying in that bed, he would definitely want to see him.

The thought gave rise to another upsurge of emotion and he hurriedly excused himself. He checked with Sofia that all was well then went to his office. The couch pulled out into a bed but he couldn't be bothered setting it up and simply lay down. He ached with tiredness but it was a good kind of tiredness, one that stemmed from a job well done. Once again the thought that he was wasting his talents struck him and he knew that he needed to rethink his plans for the future.

He sighed. There were an awful lot of things he needed to think about as well as the direction his career should take. When would Amy decide what she intended to do about Jacob? They had been interrupted by last night's emergency but he needed to know if she was willing to allow him to play a role in Jacob's life now that she knew about his heart attack. He also needed to know if she felt any differently about *him* even though he wasn't sure why it should matter. His main concern had to be Jacob, surely?

* * *

Philo's elderly parents were in the dining room when Amy took Jacob for breakfast the following morning. They had been drafted in to cover for their son and daughter-in-law who were still at the hospital. Although they spoke very little English, through a series of mimes Amy was able to deduce that Yanni had come through the operation extremely well. She expressed her relief then went to pour her and Jacob a glass of orange juice each. Donna Roberts was at the buffet and she pulled a face when she saw Amy.

'I don't think much of the choice this morning, do you? There's only one type of bread and no jam, just this honey.' She poked at the pot of local honey as though it was something revolting rather the delicious confection it actually was.

'I don't suppose Philo's parents have had time to sort things out,' Amy said soothingly, helping herself to some of the bread. 'It must have been hectic, what with Yanni's accident and ev-

erything. You do know about that, don't you?'
she added as an afterthought.

'Oh, yes.' Donna picked up a fig and poked
her fingernail into it. She put it back in the dish
and sighed. 'Tim and I saw the ambulance when
we were coming back from the *taverna* and then
Harvey told us that Yanni had cut himself. He
was here, you see, and had a ringside seat.'

'Harvey was here on his own!' Amy exclaimed.

'*Yes*. He's almost ten and well able to amuse
himself for a couple of hours while we go out,'
Donna retorted. She went back to her table, obviously not appreciating the fact that Amy had
seen fit to question her childcare arrangements,
or rather, the lack of them.

Amy returned to her own table, trying to tell
herself that it was none of her business how the
other family behaved, but it was hard to ignore
what had happened. Leaving the boy on his own
was a definite no-no in her opinion, although she
wasn't sure what she should do about it. Jacob
wanted to spend the morning on the beach again

so once breakfast was finished, they made their way there. Donna and her husband and son were already there so it appeared they were going to do the same as the previous day—spend the day sunbathing and visit Darcey in the evening.

Amy determinedly turned her thoughts away from the other family as she helped Jacob build a sandcastle. They had almost finished when Harvey came racing over and leapt on top of it. Jacob's face crumpled in dismay and Amy immediately sprang to his defence.

'You are a naughty boy,' she told Harvey but her words had no effect whatsoever. Sticking out his tongue, he jumped up and down on the sand-castle, trampling it underfoot.

Taking hold of Jacob's hand, Amy led him away. There was no point remonstrating with the boy when it obviously wouldn't have any effect. She gathered up their belongings and went back to the hotel, wondering what she could do to take Jacob's mind off what had happened. There was a ferry trip to some caves that she had planned to take him on as a treat and it would be the per-fect day for it.

They hurriedly changed and went to catch the bus. The ferry left from the harbour and they were just in time. Jacob loved being on the boat and especially loved it when they saw some dol-phins swimming alongside. The caves were spec-tacular too, enormous great chambers which the sea had carved out of the cliffs and filled with an eerie green light given off by the plankton that lived in the water. Jacob was entranced and took lots of photographs to show his friends when they got home. Amy's heart lightened when he told her that. Jacob seemed to have forgotten about the bullying that had made his life such a misery. Maybe she didn't need to tell him about Nico being his father, after all?

The thought stayed with her as they sailed back to the harbour. It was tempting to leave things the way they were, but she knew deep down that she was taking the coward's way out. It was eas-ier not to say anything but what if the bullying started again and she was forced to tell Jacob the truth? He would be both upset and bewildered because she hadn't told him who Nico was when she had had the chance and it would make the situation even more difficult.

She sighed. There was only a week of their holiday left and she would have to make up her mind soon.

Nico got through his morning list with very few problems. There were a couple of tourists suffering from sunburn although their injuries weren't serious. He advised them to drink plenty of water and stay in the shade. Aloe vera cream, available from the local pharmacy, would help to soothe the burns but they would be well advised to keep covered up for the remainder of their holiday. They thanked him politely but they looked very glum when they left. Keeping out of the sun obviously wasn't high on their list of priorities when they had come away on holiday.

Once surgery ended, he went straight to the

hospital. Yanni's bed had been partitioned off from the main part of the ward to afford him some peace and quiet. He was wide awake, however, when Nico arrived.

'*Kalimera*, Yanni. You look a lot better this morning, I must say.'

'I feel better,' Yanni replied, smiling shyly. He was a rather reserved young man who was studying archaeology at Athens University. He had come home for the holidays to help out at the family's hotel.

'Good.' Nico pulled up a chair. 'I'm not sure what your parents have told you but I think it's best if you know exactly what I needed to do last night.' He briefly outlined the procedure he had used to repair Yanni's arm. 'You will find that your arm is very stiff and unresponsive at first. However, I'm confident that it will improve with time and the appropriate physiotherapy.'

'So I will still be able to use it?' Yanni asked anxiously. 'Obviously, I'll need two good arms if I hope to become an archaeologist. I won't be able to go on a dig if I'm…well, handicapped in some way.'

'It will take time,' Nico told him truthfully because Yanni needed to know exactly what he was up against. 'And you'll need to follow an extremely gruelling physiotherapy programme if you hope to regain full mobility in your arm—I shall contact the head of physiotherapy at the hospital on the mainland today and make arrangements for them to see you. However, I'm confident that it can be done as long as you are determined enough.'

'There's no question about that,' Yanni told him quietly. 'I'll do whatever it takes, Dr Leonides.'

'In that case, then I'm sure you won't have a problem.'

Nico smiled his approval then left Yanni to mull over what he had said. However, he was convinced the boy would succeed and it was good to know that he had played a major part in his recovery. All of a sudden he realised that the tentative plans he had made to help other people in a similar position needed to be firmed up. It was a waste of his training and experience to give up surgery, although it would mean making some changes to his life. If he was working on the mainland several days a week, he would need to find someone to take charge of the day-to-day running of the clinic.

He sighed, aware that he had been coasting for the past couple of years. His confidence had been badly shaken when he had suffered that heart attack and he had taken the easy way out by turning his back on surgery. Now it was time to get back into the fray, although he had no intention of putting himself under the kind of pressure he had been under before. Nevertheless, it would be good to pick up the threads again. He would feel more like himself, more like the man Amy had known nine years ago.

Nico frowned. How much of his desire to return to surgery could be attributed to his need to convince Amy that he was no less of a man than he had been? He had no idea but he knew that it had played a major part in his decision and it worried him. At the end of the day, returning to surgery might make no difference whatsoever to the way Amy viewed him. And it might make no difference either to what she decided to do about Jacob. He would be well advised to bear both those points in mind. It could save him a great deal of heartache.

Jacob chattered non-stop about what they had seen on the journey back to their hotel. As soon as they got into their room, he begged Amy to let him see the photographs he had taken so she loaded them onto her iPad and left him to look at them while she took a shower. Once she was dressed, she went back into the room expecting to find him still poring over the pictures, but he was nowhere to be seen. Hurrying outside, she came to a dead stop when she found him sitting on the terrace with Nico. They had their heads bent over the iPad and her heart ached when she saw them. Jacob looked so like Nico that it was uncanny.

Nico looked round and smiled when he heard her footsteps but Amy could see the wariness in his eyes. Was he worried about the reception he would receive by turning up unannounced? Or was he more concerned about what she had decided to tell Jacob? After all, it couldn't be easy for him to acknowledge Jacob as his son when he had made it clear in the past that he hadn't wanted children. It was hard to hide how much that thought hurt as she sat down beside them.

'Nico said that he's been *swimming* in these caves!' Jacob looked up, his face alight with excitement as he held up the iPad for her to see. 'How cool is that, Mum?'

'Very cool,' Amy replied, trying and failing to maintain a neutral tone. She saw Nico look at her and hurried on, wanting to deflect his attention away from her. She knew how he felt about having children and it was silly to feel hurt. 'Maybe you can do the same one day.'

'Can I? Really?' Jacob shot to his feet. 'When?'

'I…erm…I'm not sure,' she replied, wishing she hadn't said that. 'You're not allowed to swim from the boat—they told us that. And I have no idea how you can get to the caves any other way.'

'I bet Nico knows, don't you, Nico?'

Amy swallowed her groan of dismay as Jacob turned imploringly to Nico. She knew where this was leading but before she could say anything to defuse the situation, Nico replied.

'Yes. In fact, I can drive you there, if you like. There's a very strong undercurrent where the boats anchor which is why they don't allow visitors to swim there. However, you can swim closer in to the land. It's quite safe there.'

'Brill! So when can we go? Tomorrow?'

Amy sighed. Now that Jacob had heard that he wouldn't give up, and the thought of him *coercing* Nico into driving them to the caves didn't sit easily with her. 'I expect Nico is busy tomorrow, sweetheart. After all, he isn't on holiday like us.

He can't just go swanning off when he has patients to see.'

'Actually, I'm free tomorrow afternoon as it happens. I usually try to catch up with any paperwork that needs my attention but it can wait.' He looked calmly back at her, giving no indication as to his true feelings. 'I'd be happy to drive you and Jacob to the caves.'

'Oh, I couldn't let you do that,' she protested, desperately trying to come up with a bona fide reason to refuse the offer. After all, it wasn't as though he had made it willingly when he had been more or less *forced* into it.

'Why not? I could do with some R & R and I can't think of anything I'd enjoy more than swimming in the caves. It's very soothing, believe me. I'm sure you'd enjoy it too, Amy.'

His tone was so bland that Amy couldn't understand why a wave of heat flashed through her body. Nico wasn't inviting them along because he wanted to spend time with *her*, she told herself sternly, but it was hard to accept that. There was just something about the way he was looking at her, his deep brown eyes holding a light that she hadn't seen in them for a very long time…

She blanked out that foolish thought as Jacob started to perform a happy dance across the terrace. It was obvious how thrilled he was at the thought of the forthcoming trip and all of sudden she didn't have the heart to disappoint him. 'In that case then thank you. We would love to go, wouldn't we, Jacob?'

'Yes!' Jacob roared at full throttle.

Amy grimaced as he went racing inside. 'You've made one little boy very happy from the sound of it.'

Nico laughed. 'We aim to please.' He sobered abruptly. 'I hope I didn't push you into it, though, Amy. That was the last thing I intended to do.'

'Of course not.' She fixed a smile to her mouth, not wanting him to guess that she had reservations. She was very aware that the more time Jacob spent with Nico, the more he would grow to like him. It was what was happening to her, after all. Whenever she spent time with Nico, she found herself liking him more than ever.

It was a disturbing thought so it was a relief when Nico got up to leave. At the end of the day it didn't matter how she felt, she reminded herself. This was all about Jacob and how it would affect him if he found out that Nico was his father. Should she tell him or should she keep it a secret for a while longer?

It should have been easy to know what to do, but meeting Nico again had changed everything, especially in light of what he had told her about his heart attack. Would it be wise to allow Jacob to grow to love him when there was a chance that Nico might not be around to watch him growing up? The thought was so painful that it was hard to hide how devastated it made her feel when Nico turned to her. Maybe her feelings didn't count, but she couldn't bear to imagine a world where he no longer existed.

'I'll be off then. I only called in to have a word with Darcey's parents. She was discharged this afternoon and I wanted to make sure that her parents understand how important it is that she stays out of the sun for the rest their holiday. However, it appears that they've gone out for the evening.'

'Oh, I see.' Amy frowned. 'Let's hope they've got the sense to follow instructions.'

'Let's hope so,' he agreed, glancing round as though he was eager to leave.

'Well, thanks again,' she said hastily, not wanting to delay him. Maybe he had plans for the evening, she mused, plans that included dinner with an attractive female companion. After all, Nico was a very handsome and personable man and there must be lots of women eager to spend time with him. The thought was depressing and she hurried on. 'It's really kind of you to offer to drive us to those caves tomorrow. I do appreciate it.'

'It's my pleasure.' He smiled at her and once again she felt heat roar through her when she saw the warmth in his eyes. It seemed like the most natural thing in the world when he bent and kissed her lightly on the lips. *'Kalispera*, Amy. Until tomorrow.'

'Kalispera,' she murmured, her heart racing as she watched him walk away. He disappeared from sight and a moment later she heard a car engine roar to life. Only then did she start to breathe again.

Amy touched a fingertip to her mouth, feeling the heat that Nico's lips had left behind. The kiss may have been meant as no more than a token gesture but it didn't feel like that, not when her mouth was burning this way. Panic suddenly engulfed her as she realised just how precarious the situation was. She couldn't afford to let her judgement be clouded by emotion, couldn't allow herself to be swayed by desire. She had to do what was right for Jacob and not what *she* wanted.

She groaned. What she wanted more than anything at that moment was Nico holding her, kissing her, *making love* to her, and it was foolish to wish for such things. Nico had done all of that nine years ago—kissed her, held her, made passionate love to her—but it hadn't meant anything, had it? Why should she imagine that it would mean anything now? Why should she even care? The answers to those questions hovered at the back of her mind but she was too afraid to search them out. It was safer—much safer—to leave them where they were.

CHAPTER NINE

NICO TOOK A deep breath as he drew up outside the hotel the following afternoon. He had found it impossible to rid himself of the memory of that kiss. Maybe it had started out as a mere token gesture yet it had filled his mind to the point where it had required a huge amount of effort to focus on his patients' needs all morning long.

That was something which had never happened to him before. Work had *always* taken priority in the past. However, every time he had relaxed his guard, he had found himself recalling how sweet Amy's lips had tasted, how seductive; how much he wanted to kiss her again! Now he could only pray that he wouldn't do something foolish. Maybe Amy hadn't pushed him away last night but there was no reason to think that she wanted him to kiss her again.

He dismissed that depressing thought as he went into the hotel. Helena was behind the reception desk and he saw the colour drain from her face when she saw him coming in and silently cursed himself. 'Yanni is fine,' he said hastily. 'I saw him shortly before I left the clinic and he was sitting up and chatting to one of the other patients.'

'Oh, thank heavens!' Helena pressed a hand to her heart. 'We have guests arriving today so I stayed behind to get everything ready while Philo went to visit him. I thought it must be bad news when I saw you.'

'On the contrary, Yanni is making excellent progress. In fact, if he carries on like this he should be able to come home next week.'

'Really? Oh, that is good news!' Helena exclaimed. She looked past him and smiled broadly. 'Dr Leonides has just told me that Yanni might be able to come home next week. Isn't that wonderful news?'

'It is indeed.'

Nico felt the skin on the back of his neck prickle when he recognised Amy's voice. He turned slowly around, doing his best not to react when he saw her standing behind him, but it was impossible. She was wearing another sundress in the palest shade of pink. It had narrow straps which tied at the shoulders and a scooped neckline that immediately drew his eyes to the curve of her breasts. She looked so lovely and so desirable that he wanted nothing more than to sweep her into his arms and kiss her until they were both senseless, but how could he do that when he had no idea if it was what she wanted too? The thought was deflating so it was a relief when Jacob came racing across the hall and almost bowled him over.

'Hey, steady on, young man,' Nico said, putting out a restraining hand. 'We don't want any more accidents, do we?'

'He's been so excited,' Amy said softly. 'I can't count the number of times he's asked me when you would be coming to collect us.'

'Well, I'm here now so we may as well get off.' Nico smoothed his face into a suitably non-committal expression. Maybe he *was* behaving irrationally but he had no intention of letting her know that. The last thing he wanted was Amy thinking that he was vulnerable in any way. 'Have you everything you need? Towels, swim-suits, et cetera?'

'I think so.' She showed him the extra-large holdall she was carrying. 'Jacob's also brought along his snorkel and mask, plus his flippers. He obviously intends to make the most of this trip,' she added dryly.

'Good for him!'

Nico laughed as he ruffled the boy's hair. It felt remarkably good to know that Jacob was look-ing forward to the outing so much. Children ob-viously didn't need expensive presents or lots of money spent on them: they just needed attention. Nico logged the thought for future reference as he turned to Helena. 'Sorry again about giving you such a fright. As I said, Yanni is making excellent progress and there really is no need for you to worry.'

'Thank you, Doctor,' Helena replied, glancing from him to Jacob.

Nico swallowed his sigh when he saw her expression change. It was obvious that Helena had noticed the resemblance between him and Jacob and it made him wonder how much longer Amy could keep their relationship a secret. Surely it wouldn't be long before Jacob himself became aware of it?

That thought accompanied him as he led the way to his car. Although he didn't want to force the issue, he was more convinced than ever that Amy needed to make up her mind about what she intended to do. If she planned to tell Jacob that he was his father then it would be better to get it over with as soon as possible. Quite frankly, he couldn't understand what was taking her so long…unless she was still unsure about him. After all, he had made no bones about the fact that he hadn't wanted children nine years ago, but surely she could see that he had changed?

Nico's heart started to pound as he slid into the driver's seat. Maybe he hadn't wanted a family in the past but he definitely wanted one now. He wanted to be a proper father to Jacob and he wanted it more than he had wanted anything in his entire life. It was a huge shock to realise just how important it was to him too. Now all he needed to do was to convince Amy that she could trust him.

He squared his shoulders as he started the engine. Bearing in mind everything that had happened in the past, it wasn't going to be easy to convince her, but somehow, some *way*, he intended to play a role in Jacob's life from now on!

It took them just half an hour to reach the caves. Amy had expected it to take much longer than that and wasn't prepared when Nico announced that they were there. She fixed a smile to her mouth as she got out of the car but she could feel her stomach churning with nerves.

It had been easier while they had been driving. Nico had needed to concentrate on the narrow, winding roads so she had been spared having to make conversation with him. However, now that they had arrived, she would have to play her part for Jacob's sake. Jacob would think it very strange if she didn't talk to Nico, yet the thought made her feel on edge. Maybe it was silly to keep thinking about that kiss but she couldn't help it. The memory seemed to fill every tiny corner of her mind even though she knew she mustn't allow it to influence her. She had to focus on doing what was right for Jacob and not what she wanted.

'The entrance to the caves is down there.' Nico pointed to a path leading down the side of the cliff and she hurriedly gathered her thoughts.

'It looks very steep to me. Are you sure it's safe?'

'Yes. Steps have been cut into the rock and

there's a handrail to hold on to so there shouldn't be a problem getting down.' He smiled reassuringly. 'I'll carry everything down while you keep an eye on Jacob.'

Amy nodded as she opened the back door and let Jacob out of the car. He immediately went racing towards the path but she called him back. 'Stay here until we've got everything out of the car,' she told him firmly. He pulled a face but he did as he was told, waiting impatiently while she retrieved her bag from the footwell.

'I'll take that.' Nico took it off her, grimacing as he swung it over his shoulder. 'I don't know what you've got in here but it weighs a ton!'

'Just the usual things,' she told him defensively. She held out her hand. 'I'll take it. It don't expect you to carry my bag as well as your own.'

'I don't have a bag. Only this,' Nico replied, taking a towel out of the boot of the car. He tossed it over his shoulder and grinned at her. 'I was only teasing about the bag, Amy. It's fine, really.'

'Oh.'

Amy felt the colour rush to her cheeks as she realised that she had overreacted. She hurried over to where Jacob was waiting, wishing that she wasn't so aware of Nico that even the smallest comment seemed to take on a huge significance. She wasn't normally so sensitive but it was different with Nico; *she* behaved differently when she was with him. It had been exactly the same nine years ago too and it worried her that so little had changed. Surely she shouldn't react this way after all that time?

The thought lingered as they made their way down to the beach. Amy looked around, sighing with pleasure at the sight of the turquoise-blue water lapping at the glittering white sand. They were the only people there and it was like stepping into a tiny piece of heaven.

'It's beautiful, isn't it?' Nico came and stood beside her. 'It's one of my favourite places on the island, mainly because very few people ever come here.'

'It is beautiful,' Amy murmured, shading her eyes as she stared across the glittering blue water. 'I'm sure it would be one of my favourite places too if I lived here.'

She turned towards him and felt her breath catch when she saw the way he was looking at her. There was such hunger in his eyes that she felt herself start to tremble. When he held out his hand, she took a step towards him, drawn by the longing she could see in his eyes…

'Where's the caves, Mum? I can't see them.'

Jacob's voice brought her back down to earth with a bump. Amy took a shuddering breath, fighting to control the waves of desire that were rippling through her. She knew what would have happened if she and Nico had been alone, knew that they would have made love right here on the shimmering white sand. It was what Nico wanted. And it was what she wanted too.

Nico could feel himself shaking as he fought to control the hunger that filled every cell in his body. How had that happened? he wondered dazedly as he watched Amy walk over to Jacob. One moment he had been admiring the view and the next he had been overwhelmed by the need to make love to her. What shocked him most, however, was the fact that he knew it was what Amy had wanted too.

A shudder ran through him as he stripped off his clothes. He was wearing swimming trunks beneath as it had seemed easier to come prepared rather than have to change when they got here. Amy must have had the same idea as she was in the process of taking off her dress. Nico groaned under his breath as he took stock of the modest one-piece swimsuit she was wearing under it. Although there was nothing the least revealing about the swimsuit, it certainly pushed all his buttons! His body responded in time-honoured fashion and he hurriedly grabbed hold of his towel, using it to hide his discomfort when she turned to him.

'Should I put sunscreen on Jacob or will he be safe enough without it in the caves?' she asked in a tight little voice that immediately set all his internal alarm bells ringing.

'He'll be fine without it,' Nico replied, calling himself every kind of a fool. Maybe he *did* want to make love to her, and maybe it *was* what she had wanted too, but they both knew it would be a mistake. They needed to concentrate on Jacob, on doing what was right for him. At the end of the day, Amy wouldn't want him disrupting her life when she had managed perfectly well without him for the past nine years.

It was a sobering thought and Nico knew that he must bear it in mind as he continued. 'It's best not to pollute the water with any kind of oils as it can affect the plankton that live in the caves. Anyone swimming there is advised not to use sunscreen for that reason.'

'Oh, I see.' She picked up a towel and draped it across Jacob's shoulders to protect him from the sun until they reached the caves then looked at Nico. 'We're ready whenever you are.'

'Fine. You'll need to leave your sandals on as

we have to climb over those rocks,' he told her, relieved to have something practical to focus on rather than all the conflicting thoughts and feelings that plagued him. 'Once we reach the caves, though, you can take them off as we'll be walking over sand.'

He led the way, pausing at intervals to make sure they were keeping up. They reached the entrance to the caves and he helped Jacob jump down off the rocks then turned to help Amy, feeling his breath catch when she placed her hand in his. He quickly released her once she was safely down on the sand.

'The entrance to the caves is rather low and quite narrow,' he explained, trying not to think about how small and fragile her fingers had felt when they had gripped his. 'However, it widens out after a couple of metres so it shouldn't be a problem. You're not worried about confined spaces, are you?'

'Not that I know,' she replied.

Nico's skin prickled when he heard the tension in her voice. It was obvious that she had felt something too when she had held his hand and it was all he could do not to say anything only he knew it would be a mistake. Maybe they were both incredibly aware of one another but it wasn't going to lead anywhere. They'd had their chance and it would be foolish to think they could take a step back in time. They were very different people these days and they could never recapture the feelings they'd had for one another all those years ago.

His heart was heavy as he ducked into the entrance to the caves. Even though he knew how pointless it was, he couldn't help wishing that he had behaved very differently nine years ago. If he could have the time all over again, he would never let Amy go.

CHAPTER TEN

THEY SWAM FOR almost an hour before Amy decided that she had spent enough time in the water. She got out and wrapped herself in her towel, watching as Jacob scooped up a handful of water and splashed Nico with it. He shrieked with delight when Nico picked him up and tossed him into the water, and she sighed. Although she did her best, she couldn't play with him the way Nico did. It made her see how much Jacob had missed by not having his father around.

'Right, that's it. You've worn me out, young man.' Nico waded out of the water, shaking his head when Jacob pleaded with him to go back in. 'Once I've had a rest then maybe I'll come in again. OK?'

Amazingly, Jacob accepted his decision without arguing. Amy's brows rose as Nico sat down beside her. 'I'm impressed. Jacob doesn't usually give in so easily when he wants something.'

'No?' He shrugged as he picked up his towel and started to dry himself. 'Maybe he decided I needed a break.'

Or, more likely, Jacob had realised that Nico wasn't a push-over and had reacted accordingly, she thought wryly. It was yet another point in Nico's favour, another reason why Jacob would benefit from having him around. Jacob needed a male presence in his life, a role model he could look up to. It was on the tip of her tongue to tell Nico that but she held back. Although there were many plus points to having Nico play a part in Jacob's life there were minuses too, the biggest one being the matter of his health. Although he appeared to be as fit as ever, she couldn't ignore what he had told her about the increased risk of him having another heart attack. She couldn't bear to imagine Jacob's anguish if anything happened to him. She couldn't bear to imagine her own anguish either.

Amy lay back on her towel, closing her eyes while she tried to deal with the thought. She knew without the shadow of a doubt that she would be devastated if anything happened to him yet she didn't understand why. After all, he hadn't been part of her life for a very long time. She hadn't seen or spoken to him for nine long years, in fact. Admittedly, she had thought about him frequently during that time but that was only to be expected when Jacob was a constant reminder of Nico's existence. In truth it shouldn't make a scrap of difference what happened to Nico, but she knew in her heart that her world would fall apart if he died.

It was a shock to have to face up to that fact, so it was a relief when Nico announced a short time later that it was time they left. Amy helped Jacob dry himself after he reluctantly waded out of the water then she quickly gathered up their belongings. She desperately needed a breathing space, time on her own to get her thoughts into some sort of order. Being around Nico only seemed to confuse her and that was the last thing she needed when she still had to decide what to do about Jacob. She still wasn't sure that telling him Nico was his father would be a good idea.

Nico glanced around, checking that they hadn't left anything behind. There was a rusty drinks can wedged into a crevice in the rocks and he picked it up. 'Somebody must have tossed it over the side of a boat. They don't realise the damage they can cause by not taking their litter home with them. Things like this—cans and plastic bottles—are a real hazard for the local sea life.'

'There's always someone who can't be bothered to clear up after themselves,' Amy agreed then stopped when she heard shouting. 'Did you hear that? It seemed to be coming from one of the other caves.'

'It did.' Nico's expression was grim as he turned and made his way along the narrow strip of sand that bordered the water.

Amy followed him, keeping tight hold of Jacob's hand in case he slipped into the water.

There were several more caves leading off from the one they had swum in but Nico had told her that it wasn't safe to swim in them. Apparently, there were strong currents flowing through them which could catch an unwary bather off guard. They came to the entrance to the largest of the caves and stopped. Nico shook his head when they heard people shouting.

'It sounds as though someone is in difficulty. I'd better see what's happened.'

With that he ducked into the cave and disappeared. Amy hesitated but there was no way that she was letting him go on his own. She turned to Jacob, wanting to impress on him just how serious this was. 'We're going to go with Nico but you are *not* to go into the water. Do you understand?'

Jacob nodded. He looked decidedly scared as they followed Nico into the cave. Amy gave his hand a reassuring squeeze, hoping that she was doing the right thing. She didn't want to frighten him but, equally, she didn't want to leave Nico to deal with this on his own. She sighed. Talk about being trapped between a rock and a hard place!

The cave was much bigger than the one they had swum in. It was also a lot brighter as it led directly out to sea. Amy had to wait while her eyes adjusted to the light then gasped as she took in the scene. There was someone in the water, a teenaged boy from what she could tell, and he was obviously in difficulty. She could see a boat anchored close to the mouth of the cave and recognised it as the same boat she and Jacob had sailed on the previous day. She could only assume that the teenager had either jumped or fallen off the boat. The crew were in the process of lowering a dinghy into the water but it was doubtful if they would reach him in time. The current kept dragging him under and her heart plummeted as he disappeared from sight once more.

'I'm going to swim out there and keep him afloat until the dinghy gets to him.'

Nico waded into the water before Amy could

say anything. She pressed a hand to her mouth as she watched him start to swim out to the teenager because it was obvious that he was having problems with the current too. He finally reached the boy just as he was dragged under again and she cried out in alarm when she saw Nico dive beneath the waves. It seemed to take for ever before he surfaced, holding the boy with one arm as he struggled to keep them both afloat. The dinghy was in the water now and she held her breath, praying that Nico's strength would hold out long enough for it to reach them.

The boy was finally hauled into the dinghy and then the crew helped Nico in as well and brought him back to where she and Jacob were waiting. He jumped out, pausing briefly to instruct the crew to take the teenager straight to the clinic once they arrived back at the harbour. Amy handed him her towel, unable to put into words how she felt. She had been so scared when she had seen him disappear beneath the waves…

Tears filled her eyes and she turned away but not quickly enough to stop him seeing them.

'Amy? What is it? What's wrong?' He bent to look at her, but she shook her head.

'Nothing. I'm fine.' She glanced at Jacob. 'That boy was very silly to try to swim in this cave, wasn't he?'

'Yes.' Jacob turned to Nico and there was an expression of hero worship on his face. 'It was really cool the way you dived under the water and saved him.'

'If I hadn't done so then I'm sure someone else would have done it,' Nico said lightly. He ruffled Jacob's hair. 'Anyway, that's quite enough excitement for one day, young man. It's time I took you and your mum back to your hotel.'

'Oh, do we have to go back to the hotel? Can't we go to your house?' Jacob pleaded. 'We could go fishing again!'

'Not today,' Amy said firmly. 'Nico has spent enough time entertaining us. Anyway, I'm sure he would appreciate some peace and quiet after what's just happened.'

'On the contrary, I would love some company.' Nico's voice was soft and deep. It stroked along her raw nerves like a velvet-gloved hand and she shivered. 'There was a moment back there when I did wonder if I had been overly confident about my prowess as a swimmer. The current in that cave is extremely strong.'

Amy knew that he was telling her the truth and it placed her in a very difficult position. If she refused to go back to his house, both Jacob and Nico would be disappointed, but was it really wise to go there when her emotions were in such turmoil? Seeing Nico disappear beneath the waves had crystallised her earlier thoughts and added to them as well: she couldn't bear it if anything happened to him. She couldn't bear it because she still had feelings for him.

She bit her lip as panic assailed her. Admitting how she felt had been the easy bit—keeping it from him would be the hard part. However, no matter how she felt about Nico, she must never forget that Jacob came first. If she didn't think it was in Jacob's best interests to tell him that Nico was his father then once they left the island, they would never see him again.

Nico could feel the tension building as he drove them to his home. He had called into the clinic on the way to check on the teenager but, thankfully, the boy had seemed none the worse for his adventures. He had given him a stern talking to before he had sent him on his way and could only hope it would stop him doing anything so foolish again. All it took was one rash decision and the consequences could prove catastrophic.

He groaned under his breath when it struck him that he was a fine one to be handing out advice. If he had thought about the consequences, he would never have invited Amy to his house again tonight. Having her in his home was going to test his self-control to its absolute limit and he could only pray that he would manage to hold out. He certainly couldn't afford to think about how much he longed to take her to his bed!

Nico breathed in deeply as he drew up in front of the house, trying to contain the rush of desire that flowed through him. He got out of the car and waited while Amy helped Jacob out of the back. She turned and he could tell at once how nervous she was and was overwhelmed by sudden tenderness. No matter how hard it was, he would always protect her, he vowed. He had hurt her once before and he would make sure that he never hurt her again, no matter what the cost was to him personally. And if that meant him stepping out of her and Jacob's lives then that was what he would do.

Amy finished preparing the salad and placed the bowl in the fridge to keep cool. She glanced at her watch, wondering how much longer Nico and Jacob were going to be. The sooner they came back, the sooner she and Jacob could eat their supper and leave. Even though Nico had done nothing whatsoever to alarm her, she was feeling very much on edge. If she carried on this way then Jacob could start to wonder what was wrong with her. The last thing she wanted was him thinking that she was keeping something from him, even if it were true.

'We only caught *one* fish, Mum, and Nico caught it, not me!' Jacob couldn't contain his disappointment as he burst into the house. Amy quickly set aside her qualms and adopted an upbeat expression.

'Never mind, sweetheart. You can always try again another day,' she said encouragingly, then winced. She certainly didn't want Nico thinking that she was angling for another invitation, did she?

'That's what I said.'

Nico smiled as he followed Jacob into the house, but she could sense a definite tension about him and frowned. Was he having second thoughts about them being here, wishing that he hadn't invited them? She sighed softly. Quite frankly, she wouldn't blame him if he was. After all, the situation must be no less stressful for him than it was for her. The thought made her come to a swift decision.

'Well, seeing as you haven't caught enough fish for our supper, I think we should go back to the hotel.' She shook her head when Jacob started to protest. 'No. It isn't fair to expect Nico to provide a meal for us, darling.'

'It isn't a problem,' Nico said quietly. 'There's plenty of food in the fridge so we certainly won't go hungry.'

'Please say we can stay, Mum!' Jacob pleaded. *'Please!'*

He sounded so desperate that Amy found herself wavering, even though she knew that she should insist they leave. It was the sensible thing to do, to put some space between her and Nico while she thought everything through. She couldn't afford to rush into a decision that was founded on emotion rather than solid common sense.

'It just doesn't seem right that Nico should have to cook for us again,' she began but Nico interrupted her.

'I'm not. We shall share the work and all make dinner.' He turned to Jacob before she could say anything else. 'Right, you're in charge of the pudding, young man.' He opened the refrigerator door and stepped aside. 'There's fruit, yogurt, cheese—whatever you fancy. I shall leave it up to you to decide what we have.'

'Yes!' Jacob was grinning from ear to ear as he began to plunder the contents of the fridge.

Amy groaned. 'You do realise that we'll probably end up with all his favourite food piled into one dish?'

'It can't be any worse than some of the meals I made when I first started cooking for myself,' Nico said wryly as he took cutlery out of a drawer.

'Oh, dear!' Amy laughed. 'That bad, was it?'

'Worse.' He glanced round and she could see a hint of embarrassment on his face. 'I hadn't a clue, basically. There had always been someone to cook for me in the past and I am ashamed to admit that even doing something as simple as boiling an egg was a major feat.'

'But at least you had a go. And you've obviously come on in leaps and bounds if that meal you cooked for us the last time we were here was anything to go by. It was delicious.'

'Thank you. I knew I had to make some major changes to my life after my heart attack and learning how to cook was one of them.' His tone was grave all of a sudden. Amy felt her heart start to flutter when he continued because she sensed that whatever he was about to say was important to him.

'I suppose what I'm trying to say is that I'm not the same person I was when we knew each other before, Amy. I…well, I'll understand if you view me differently these days.'

CHAPTER ELEVEN

NICO HELD HIS breath as he waited for Amy to reply. Maybe it was asking too much to expect her to declare her feelings but he couldn't help himself. He needed to know if she viewed him as less than the man he had been: the man who had been her first lover.

Heat flashed along his veins as the words awoke all sorts of memories. He had been both surprised and oddly moved when Amy had admitted that she hadn't slept with anyone before him. He had never set any store by a woman's innocence before; if he had thought about it at all then it would have seemed more of a hindrance than anything else. The sort of women he usually dated were exactly like him—independent, single-minded women who viewed sex merely as a pleasurable experience and not a prelude to a lifetime's commitment. And yet discovering that Amy had been a virgin had triggered the strangest response inside him. Not only had it felt as though she was giving him a very special gift, knowing that he was to be her first lover had been a big responsibility too. He had resolved to make the experience as wonderful for her as it could possibly be, and it had been too.

Nico shuddered as he recalled how sweetly responsive she had been to his kisses and caresses. It may have been Amy's first time but, amazingly, he had felt as though it had been his first time as well. Nothing had prepared him for the sheer depth of feeling she had evoked inside him. Why even now he could recall how he had felt that night, how aroused he had been, how much he had desired her, and it was another shock to realise that the memory of that time was as clear and as vivid as ever.

He had truly thought that he had put it all behind him but he had been wrong. Meeting Amy had been a milestone in his life and if he hadn't been so stubbornly set on proving himself then he would have recognised just how important their time together had been. He wouldn't have left her if he had. He would have stayed with her. Stayed with her and Jacob so that now they wouldn't be facing this dilemma because one thing was certain: Amy wouldn't have abandoned *him* after his heart attack. She would have remained with him, cared for him, *despite* what had happened.

Regret filled him even though Nico knew how pointless it was. He had had his chance and no amount of wishing that he had acted differently would change things. It was a relief when Amy didn't say anything because he couldn't have borne it if she had tried to be kind. He didn't want her pity. It was the last thing he wanted!

Nico took a package of lamb out of the fridge and set it on the counter with a thud. It was hard to contain his emotions but he'd had years of practice and it stood him in good stead now. Nobody would have guessed that it felt as though his heart was bleeding at the thought of what he had lost through his own stupidity.

'How about kebabs?' he suggested, blanking out any trace of emotion from his voice. Inside he might be suffering the torments of the damned but, by heaven, he wouldn't show it. 'It won't take long to prepare them and then we can cook them outside on the barbecue.'

'That would be lovely.'

Amy's voice was flat and all his senses immediately went on alert. Was she trying not to let him know how she felt? he wondered grimly. Trying to hide the fact that in her eyes he was no longer the man he had been, the lover who had aroused her passion to previously undiscovered heights? Now his body had failed him, shown that it was only too fallible, didn't she find him attractive any more?

The thought made him want to rant and rail but it wouldn't help, certainly wouldn't change things, neither her view of him nor the fact that he wasn't a perfect specimen of manhood any longer. Nico concentrated instead on preparing their supper, spearing the lamb onto long wooden skewers and rubbing it lightly with garlic and olive oil ready to cook it on the barbecue. He had already lit the fire and the smell of pine burning greeted him as he carried the skewers outside. He smiled bitterly as he tossed a handful of fresh herbs onto the embers to infuse the meat with extra flavour. If he couldn't prove his prowess as a lover then at least he could prove that he could cook a decent meal.

Amy wished with all her heart that she had said something. As they ate their supper, her mind kept returning to what Nico had said about her viewing him differently. The worst thing was that she knew it was true. She did see him in a different light but that was because he *was* different.

The Nico she had known nine years ago had been harder, more focused, far more self-centred. He had changed a lot and whether it was because of his heart attack or what, there was no denying it. How could she have claimed that her view of him hadn't altered, especially when nine years ago she had been madly, crazily in love with him? It would have been tantamount to admitting that she still felt the same way about him today.

Her heart knocked painfully against her ribs and she bent over her plate, spearing the last tender morsel of lamb with her fork. She popped it into her mouth then turned to check that Jacob was eating his supper. Her eyes slid over Nico, stopping abruptly when she realised that he was watching her, and she felt her heart give another of those painful leaps when she saw the expression on his face, a mixture of pure longing and intense regret…

She turned away, her breath coming in tight little spurts as she helped Jacob to cut up the last few pieces of his kebab. She wasn't sure what had prompted the regret on Nico's face but she understood only too well what had provoked that longing. Nico wanted her. He wanted her as a man wanted a woman he found attractive. It was only too easy to understand how he felt when it was how she felt too.

It was a relief when they all finished their main course and Jacob hurried inside to fetch the pudding as it provided a welcome distraction. He came back and carefully placed the bowls on the table, looking as pleased as punch. Amy stared at the assortment in front of her, unsure what to say. Yogurt, some mangled-looking figs, several great dollops of honey, all topped off with chunks of feta cheese made for an eclectic dessert.

'Mmm, this looks interesting.'

She glanced up when Nico spoke, watching as he picked up his spoon and dipped it into his bowl. Was she still in love with him after all this time and everything that had happened? Oh, admittedly she felt *something* for him but something was a long way from being love, surely? How could love survive without any encouragement? Without any reason to hope that it would be reciprocated? Surely, the way they had parted had killed the love she had had for Nico stone dead?

Amy struggled to reason it out and yet the harder she tried, the less sure she was. If she had felt nothing at all for him then it would have been easier but there was no point lying to herself. She felt something for him and only time would tell exactly what it was.

Nico finished loading the dirty dishes into the dishwasher. Night was drawing in and the lanterns he had placed around the terrace provided a soft glow in the encroaching darkness. He watched as Amy picked up her glass and drank the last of her wine. It was time he drove her and Jacob back to their hotel and yet he hated the thought of them leaving. If it had been up to him they would have stayed the night but he knew it wouldn't be wise. If Amy stayed then they would end up in bed together and that was the last thing he should allow to happen, even though he knew it was what she wanted as much as he did. However, allowing desire to dictate their actions was a recipe for disaster.

A gust of wind suddenly blew in from the sea and Nico saw one of the patio chairs topple over. He hurried outside and quickly righted it, frowning when he felt the first drops of rain start to fall. It rarely rained at this time of the year and when it did, it usually heralded one of the violent storms that occasionally swept over the island. If he was to return Amy and Jacob to their hotel then they needed to set off straight away.

'I'm sorry to cut the evening short but I really need to drive you back before the storm sets in,' he explained. 'These summer storms can be incredibly fierce and I don't want us to get halfway there and end up stranded.'

'Of course.' Amy hurriedly stood up, making a grab for her chair as another gust of wind threatened to blow it over. 'That wind came from nowhere!' she exclaimed, tucking the chair under the marble-topped table.

'It did,' Nico agreed, quickly gathering up the lanterns and carrying them inside. 'That's why it's so dangerous. One minute everything is as calm as can be and the next moment the wind springs up. A lot of fishing boats have been lost because of it.'

'How awful!'

Amy shuddered as she followed him inside and Nico sighed. He had forgotten how tender-hearted she was and hated to think that he might have upset her.

'Most of the fishing boats will be safely moored in the harbour by now,' he assured her. 'Very few boats go night fishing these days, mainly because the sea around the island is so difficult to navigate. There are too many partly submerged rocks to take the risk.'

'That's good to know.' She gave him a quick smile then went through to the sitting room where Jacob was playing on his games console.

Nico made sure the candles in the lanterns were safely snuffed out then found his car keys.

The rain was beating down now so he went into the hall and dug out a couple of rarely used waterproof jackets from the cupboard. Amy and Jacob would get soaked if they didn't put something over their clothes.

'Here. Put these on,' he instructed when they appeared. He held up a jacket so that Jacob could slip his arms into it. It was way too large for the child but Nico zipped it up anyway and pulled the hood over Jacob's head.

'Your turn,' he said, turning to Amy. He held the jacket while she slid her arms into the sleeves then automatically started to zip it up just as he had done for Jacob. His fingers brushed against the soft curve of her breast and he felt a rush of heat pour through him at the accidental contact.

'It's all right. I can manage, thank you.'

She stepped away from him, making a great production out of zipping the jacket the rest of the way and pulling up the hood, but he could see that her hands were trembling and knew she had felt it too, felt that rush of desire that had hit him.

Nico dragged on his own jacket and led the way outside. The rain was pouring down now, huge great drops that stung their faces as they ran to the car, but he was barely aware of the storm raging around them. Quite frankly it couldn't compete with the storm that was raging inside him. He wanted Amy so much! Wanted her with a passion that belied all reason. It was as though every atom of his being had been consumed by this need to make love to her again.

Was it simply because it had been a while since he had made love to a woman? he wondered as he helped Jacob scramble into the back of the car. He wanted to believe that was the true explanation, but there was no point lying to himself. It was only Amy he wanted, only Amy who could arouse his desire to this extent. And it was such a devastatingly profound thought that his heart seemed to scrunch up inside him. Even if he could never have her, he would always want her.

Amy sat on the edge of her seat as Nico drove them along the narrow winding road. It took all his skill to keep them on course as the wind roared around them but in truth it wasn't the storm that scared her but what had happened before they had left his house. She had felt it too, felt that surge of desire that had passed between them when he had accidentally touched her breast, and it simply confirmed her worst fears. Making a decision about Nico's involvement in Jacob's life would be all the more difficult when her emotions were in such turmoil.

'What the devil...?'

Amy was roused abruptly from her thoughts when Nico slammed on the brakes. Peering through the windscreen she could see that the road ahead was blocked by boulders which had tumbled down off the mountainside. Nico turned to her and his expression was grave.

'Stay here while I check to see if we can get past, although I doubt it. It looks like the whole road has been blocked.'

Amy bit her lip as he got out of the car, bending almost double as he fought his way against the wind. He had almost reached the landslide when there was an almighty roar and more rocks started to roll down onto the carriageway. Instinctively she went to get out of the car to make sure he was all right but he was already heading back.

'Get in.' He slammed her door then hurried round to the driver's side. 'We need to get away from here as quickly as possible,' he told her tersely as he started to back up the car. He found a turning place and turned the vehicle around, picking up speed as he drove them away from the danger point. He didn't slow down again until they came to a section where the road widened out.

'I'm afraid you won't be able to go back to your hotel tonight.' He glanced at her, his expression impossible to read in the glow from the dashboard lights. 'You and Jacob will have to stay at my house until they manage to clear the road.'

'How…how long will it take?' Amy asked, her voice barely above a whisper.

'I've no idea.' Nico shrugged but she could see his knuckles gleaming through his skin as he gripped the steering wheel. 'It all depends if that is the only landslide or if there are others further along the way. It could be a few hours or a few days before they manage to clear it all away.'

Amy swallowed, trying to dislodge the knot of panic that seemed to be constricting her throat. A few hours she could cope with, but a few days… Closing her eyes, she did her best to calm herself down but it was a losing battle from the outset. The thought of spending several days in Nico's house was daunting, especially in her present frame of mind. Could she behave sensibly or would temptation prove too much? Too much for both of them?

Opening her eyes, she shot a glance sideways at him and felt her heart give a little jolt compounded of both fear and excitement. Who knew what might happen if she and Nico were forced to spend several days together.

CHAPTER TWELVE

'YOU SHOULD BE comfortable enough in here. I'm afraid there isn't a lot by the way of furniture—I haven't got round to furnishing all the bedrooms yet. However, there is an en suite bathroom if you or Jacob need to use it during the night.'

Nico opened the door to what would eventually become a guest bedroom, stepping aside when Amy came forward to take a look.

'It's lovely. Thank you.'

She dredged up a smile but Nico could tell how on edge she felt and couldn't blame her either. The very air seemed to be thick with tension as it pulsated around them and he knew that if it weren't for the fact that Jacob was standing there beside them, he and Amy would be behaving very differently at this moment. He certainly

wouldn't be pretending to be the perfect host—
that was certain!

Desire twisted his guts, turned them to red-
hot liquid fire, and he groaned under his breath.
For a man who had always prided himself on
being in control of his emotions it was humbling
to find himself at their beck and call. He took
a deep breath, forcing himself to get a grip. He
couldn't give in to these feelings; it wouldn't be
right. Amy had to be free to decide if she wanted
him in Jacob's life without him employing some
kind of *emotional* blackmail. The thought steadied him.

'Good. I'll just fetch some sheets and make up
the bed for you.'

He half turned to leave but Amy stopped him
by placing her hand lightly on his arm. It was
the sort of instinctive gesture that anyone might
have made but there was no doubting that it had
a galvanising effect on both of them. Nico grit-
ted his teeth when he felt desire surge through
him once more, felt it flood into every atom of

his being. There wasn't a tiny, minuscule bit of him that didn't want to drag her into his arms, hold her, kiss her, let their bodies become one—

'If you'll show me where everything's kept then I'll sort out the bed.' She removed her hand and the moment passed, although Nico could see a matching desire in her eyes before she turned away. 'I don't expect you to wait on us while we're here, Nico. Really I don't.'

'In that case the linen is in here.'

He had no idea how he managed to carry it off, how he could behave as though everything was completely normal when it was so far from being that. He led the way to the huge old-fashioned linen press that had been installed when the farmhouse had been built. It stretched from floor to ceiling, the cedar wood shelves as smooth as glass after so many years of use.

'Help yourself to whatever you need,' he said, gesturing towards the beautifully ironed piles of linen. He had drawn the line at doing his own laundry and one of the women from the village did it for him. He saw Amy inhale appreciatively as she lifted an armful of sheets off a shelf and breathed in the intoxicating mix of fresh mountain air and lavender that infused them.

'These smell gorgeous!' She looked up and smiled at him and he felt his heart dance with pleasure when he saw the delight in her eyes.

'They do, although I can't claim any credit for that. One of the local women does my laundry and it always comes back smelling wonderful.'

'Ah. So you're not completely domesticated then?' she said with a teasing little laugh that helped to dispel some of the tension.

'Sadly, no. Ironing is one skill I don't intend to master.'

He returned her smile then made himself turn away before it could become something more meaningful. He needed to be wary of that happening, careful not to allow a shared moment of pleasure to take on an even greater significance. Who knew how long Amy would need to stay here? He simply couldn't afford to lower his guard and allow his emotions to dictate his actions.

'I shall leave you to sort everything out. There's blankets in the cupboard as well as towels so take whatever you need. I'll make some more coffee. I'm sure you could do with a cup. I know I could.'

His tone was brisk and far more in keeping with how he needed to behave throughout his guests' unplanned sojourn. Amy followed his lead because she too sounded much more detached and perversely Nico found himself regretting the change of mood. Foolish or not but he missed the feeling of intimacy that had surrounded them just moments earlier.

'Coffee would be very welcome. Thank you.'

Nico inclined his head then went to the kitchen and set about preparing the coffee. It was a simple enough task but he gave it his undivided attention—carefully measuring the coffee into the pot, adding hot, not boiling, water and heating the milk. Although he preferred his coffee black, Amy liked hot milk in hers...

Bam! That was all it took, just the thought of her likes and dislikes, and his mind was off and running again. Nico gripped hold of the worktop as he was assailed by a whole flood of memories: Amy's nose wrinkling as she added milk to her coffee and inhaled its aroma; her mouth pursing as she took a first tentative sip; the taste of coffee on her lips when he leant forward and kissed her...

Nico clung to the worktop as his legs threatened to buckle beneath him. He couldn't believe that the scene was so sharp and so clear. He wasn't just remembering what had happened in some abstract and distant fashion: he was reliving it. He could actually taste the coffee as it had tasted all those years ago, hot and rich, imbued with the natural sweetness of Amy's lips. It was so real that it was difficult not to believe it was actually happening right here, right now, this very second. Would it be the same if he re-enacted the scene? Would his blood quicken as he watched Amy lift the cup to her mouth, watched her lips purse in readiness to taste it? Would he be filled with the same desperate urge to kiss her as he had felt then?

A groan escaped him. Of course he would!

Amy finished tucking in the sheets and stepped back to admire her handiwork. Every corner was precisely folded, each wrinkle carefully smoothed out. It was the perfect example of how a bed *should* be made but, best of all, making it had helped to use up several potentially danger-ous minutes.

She sighed softly as she went to the old-fash-ioned dressing table and peered into the mirror. The glass was foxed with age so that her reflec-tion wasn't as clear as it could have been but that was a blessing. Opening her bag, she took out a comb and ran it through her hair, trying not to think about what Nico might see in her eyes at that moment. Desire? Definitely. A worrying lack of self-control? Almost certainly.

She couldn't remember the last time she had felt so conflicted by her emotions. Her head was telling her to get a grip and she was listening— truly she was! However, her heart was sending out an entirely different message, one that was far too beguiling to ignore: would it really matter if she gave in to her feelings, did what she longed to do and slept with Nico again? If she accepted that it must be a one-off and didn't mean anything, then what harm would there be in indulging herself for once?

After all she was a grown woman, a mother, someone who held down a highly responsible job, not some innocent young girl who didn't understand the facts of life. If she had needs like any other woman then why not do what most women would do in the circumstances, sleep with Nico and satisfy this hunger that was gnawing away inside her? No one would blame her. No one would know. They could spend the night together and enjoy one another's bodies without the world coming to an end, surely?

Amy stared into her own eyes and saw the growing temptation that shimmered in their depths but somehow she had to find the strength to fight it. Maybe another woman could have slept with Nico and walked away afterwards without any regrets but she couldn't. She would be haunted for ever by what she had done and she couldn't bear to think that her life and, more importantly, Jacob's might be affected by her actions. If she slept with Nico then she could never be sure if she had allowed any decision she made to be influenced by desire rather than common sense, could she? At the end of the day it wasn't her needs that were paramount but her son's. She had to do what was right for Jacob. Nobody else.

Turning away from the mirror, Amy made for the door. Jacob was in the kitchen with Nico when she tracked him down. He had an empty glass in his hand and a rim of milk around his mouth. Amy fixed her face into a suitably amused expression as she went to join them. There was no way that she wanted Jacob picking up on her mood and worrying.

'No need to ask what you've been up to, young man. I only hope you haven't drunk all Nico's milk. He's a real milk fiend,' she explained politely for Nico's benefit. 'I can't keep up with him when we're at home. I'm always running out.'

'There's no need to worry about that here,' Nico answered evenly. 'One of the local farmers keeps me well supplied with milk, although it's goats' milk, not cows'. There's no cattle on the island—the terrain isn't suitable for them. Although cows' milk is imported and served in most of the hotels, the locals prefer goats' milk.'

'Really!' Amy exclaimed. 'And you liked it, did you, Jacob?'

'Uh-huh. Nico said I could try it. It tasted a bit funny at first but it was OK,' Jacob replied nonchalantly. When he asked if he could go and watch television, she readily agreed, still surprised by his easy acceptance of the different milk.

'You seem surprised, Amy. Why? Is Jacob a faddy eater normally?'

'Not really.' She gave a little shrug, trying to batten down her heart which seemed to want to perform somersaults all of a sudden. If she was to stay in Nico's house until the road was reopened then she would have to talk to him, she told herself sternly. However, there was no denying that the sound of his deeply mellifluous voice was playing havoc with her willpower.

'Like most children he has his likes and dislikes but he's pretty good about trying new things. It's just that with milk being one of his absolute favourite things to drink, I was a bit surprised that he would enjoy something different.'

'Maybe it's his Greek genes coming to the fore,' Nico suggested. He laughed. 'I've always loved goats' milk so Jacob must take after me.'

'Probably.'

Amy laughed as well although the thought that it was yet another thing the pair had in common was a poignant one. As Nico busied himself pouring their coffee she couldn't help thinking how wrong it would be to keep him and Jacob apart. Maybe she did have concerns but were they really grounds enough to withhold the truth from Jacob? Surely he had a right to know that Nico was his father despite what might happen in the future?

Amy sighed as once again she found herself beset by the same old questions; however, at some point soon she would have to make up her mind what she intended to do. There was less than a week of their holiday left and if she wanted Jacob to know who Nico was then she needed to tell him before they left the island. It would give the child a chance to talk to Nico which was vital if they were to form the basis for their future relationship.

A shiver danced down her spine as she glanced over at Nico who was in the process of adding hot milk to her coffee. If she told Jacob the truth then she and Nico would also need to establish some rules for their own relationship.

Nico couldn't sleep. Whether it was all the coffee he had drunk he didn't know, but after an hour spent tossing and turning in his bed, he finally admitted defeat. Getting up he went to the window and opened the French doors, breathing in the rain-washed purity of the night air. It was just gone midnight and although the storm had started to die down, the sea was still very rough, huge white-topped breakers pounding against the shore. From where he stood, he could just make out the glimmer of the lights around the harbour and sighed.

Once the aftermath of the storm had been cleared away, everything would go back to normal and people would resume their daily routines. He would too although it wouldn't be easy to pretend that tonight had never happened. He had come so close to making love to Amy tonight and even though nothing had happened, the fact that he had wanted her so much couldn't be ignored. Of all the women he had known, Amy was the only one who affected him this way.

A sudden movement caught his eye and he turned, feeling his heart leap when he saw Amy standing on the terrace. She was still wearing the clothes she had worn that evening, making him wonder if she had even attempted to sleep. The wind was still very strong and as he watched, he saw her tip back her head so that her hair streamed out behind her like a silken banner. The effect was mesmerising.

Nico wasn't aware of moving; he wasn't aware of anything as he left his room and made his way through the house. Amy was still standing on the terrace, her eyes closed, her head tilted back, her hair twisting and turning in the wind. She couldn't have heard him approaching above the noise of the wind yet she didn't cry out when he laid his hands gently on her bare shoulders.

Maybe she had known he would come and find her. Hoped he would.

'Amy.'

The wind caught her name as soon as it left his lips and carried it away but it didn't matter. They didn't need words. They didn't need anything at that moment except each other. Nico bent and kissed the side of her neck where a pulse was beating out its own insistent rhythm, a tender, gentle kiss that would have soothed her if she had wanted soothing only that wasn't what she wanted. Her eyes opened as she turned to look at him and he could see the same questions in their depths that pounded inside his own head: *Was this right? Should they do it? Would a night of passion satisfy their hunger for one another and bring them peace?*

Stepping back, Nico held out his hand, filled with a strange sense of resignation. Maybe there were no answers to those questions. No firm negatives or positives. Only consequences. His heart trembled at the thought but it wasn't enough to make him withdraw his hand and turn away. When Amy placed her hand in his, he led her back inside, holding her lightly so that she would know that she was free to pull away if it was what she wanted. If she changed her mind.

His bedroom door was open but he paused on the threshold, giving her time, giving her space. This had to be her decision as well and not just his. When she walked past him into the room, leading him in after her, he could barely contain his joy. Even though they both understood the problems it could cause, it made no difference. They still wanted one another.

CHAPTER THIRTEEN

THE FRENCH DOORS were open, letting a flood of cool night air flow into the room. Amy could hear the waves breaking on the shore below, hear them pounding against the rocks in a rhythm that seemed to mimic the beating of her heart. Oddly enough she didn't feel afraid. For the first time in days, she knew that this was what she wanted. What she needed to do. Trying to bottle up her feelings and force them back inside her was as fruitless as trying to rebottle spilled Champagne. She had to deal with these feelings, deal with them and move on from here. If she could.

A thread of panic ran through her at that thought but it wasn't enough to make her change her mind. Nothing was. Not when Nico was standing there, behind her. She turned slowly around, letting her eyes drink in every detail.

Unlike her, he had obviously tried to go to sleep because he was wearing his nightclothes—dark grey cotton-jersey pyjama pants and a matching T-shirt that moulded the leanly muscled contours of his body. His black hair was ruffled and there was the shadow of beard darkening his jaw too. Amy felt her stomach lurch, swooping swiftly down then back up again as she realised how sexy he looked stripped of his usual formal attire. With those dark eyes staring down at her and that deeply tanned skin he was an arresting sight and she couldn't help being drawn to him.

Stepping forward, she closed the gap between them until she could feel the heat of his body seeping into hers. She was still holding his hand and she felt his fingers tighten momentarily before he deliberately loosened his grip. Did he still have doubts? she wondered as she looked into his eyes. Was he unsure about the wisdom of what they were about to do? Was he concerned about the effect it could have on Jacob or on him? More questions joined the ones that were already resident in her mind, making her feel giddy. Unsteady. Unsure.

'You don't have to do this, Amy. We don't have to do it. In fact, it would be sheer madness if we went ahead!'

The anguish in his voice was so alien that it drove everything else from her head. Amy stared at him in shock. 'You really believe that?'

'Of course I do!' He let go of her hand, his handsome face mirroring the conflict he was feeling. 'If we sleep together then it will make it that much harder for you when you make your decision about how much input I should have in Jacob's life.'

'And that's your only concern, is it?'

'No. But it has to be my main concern.' His eyes bored into hers. 'How I feel doesn't count. It's Jacob and how it could affect him that we have to focus on. I don't want you to do something you may regret in the future, Amy. That's the last thing I want.'

'Why can't this be simply a one-off?' she suggested. 'A sort of swansong rather than the start of something more.'

'And you honestly think you can treat it as that?' he said sceptically. 'You can sleep with me and then put it out of your mind?'

'Yes. Why not?' She gave a little laugh, hoping that he couldn't hear the underlying pain it held. Was that what Nico would do? Sleep with her and then forget about it afterwards? She hated the idea but could she blame him when it was what she needed to do too? 'We're both adults, Nico. We both understand that people don't need to be madly in love to enjoy having sex.'

'So that's all it would be, a means to satisfy our desire for one another?' he said slowly.

'Yes. It's obvious that we still find each other attractive so why not get it out of the way now rather than have it lurking in the background like the proverbial elephant in the room.'

He gave a deep laugh. 'Hmm, I've never heard it described that way before but maybe you're right. Maybe it would clear the air and help us both to think rationally.' He took hold of her hand and gave her a gentle tug so that she was brought into more intimate contact with him. 'I'm willing to give it a go if you are, Amy.'

Amy didn't have time to respond; she didn't have time to think even as Nico bent and claimed her mouth in a searing kiss. She kissed him back, closing her mind to the tiny voice that was telling her it was wrong, that it shouldn't be like this, that she would regret it if they made love for the wrong reasons. Who knew what was right or wrong any more? She certainly didn't! She could only follow her instincts and let them lead her down whichever path they chose.

When Nico led her to the bed, she went willingly, lying down on the cool cotton sheets that smelled of lavender. There were no lights on in the room so that everywhere was in shadow and it seemed to add to the feeling that they were cocooned in their own space. Nico was a darker shadow as he stripped off his clothes and lay down beside her but even though she couldn't see him clearly, she knew every inch of his body. Her mind had logged it away, made a blueprint of it that had been tucked into a special little corner and kept safe.

Amy ran her hands over the familiar contours, marvelling at the fact that her fingers still recognised the muscles and bones, the skin and hair that covered them after all the time that had passed. Her palm skated over the scar on his upper arm—a memento from a childhood accident when he had fallen out of a tree—and she smiled. It was like rediscovering a much-loved path, one that led to such delicious pleasures.

Her fingers travelled on, delicately skimming over his chest, following the trail until she came to his hard, flat stomach where they paused. His skin was hot to the touch, hot and dry and tense. Amy could tell that he was holding his breath, that he was doing his best to contain his desire for her. Nico had always been a generous and considerate lover, wanting to give her pleasure and not just pleasure himself, and nothing had

changed in that respect, it seemed. The thought
sent a wave of tenderness washing over her and
her fingers moved on, grazing over the crispness
of hair until she could gently wrap them around
his manhood and she heard him gasp.

'Amy…!'

His voice grated with the effort it cost him
to speak and she bent and quickly covered his
mouth with hers. She didn't want to hear what
he had to say, neither arguments nor encouragement. She was doing this for her sake as well as
his. If she could slake this desire she felt for him,
reduce it to a more bearable level, then surely it
would make the situation so much easier to understand.

Her tongue snaked out, probing his lips, en-
ticing them to open for her as passion flared inside her. There was a moment when she thought
he was going to resist, when she thought that he
was having second thoughts, and then the next
second he was rolling her over onto her back,
his powerful body pinning her to the mattress.

His mouth was so hungry as it took hers, so demanding and yet at the same time so giving that she felt tears well into her eyes. Maybe they were doing this for the wrong reasons but it didn't feel like it. Not when Nico kissed her this way. Not when it felt as though he truly cared.

Moonlight bathed the room in a silvery haze. The clouds had blown away and the sky beyond the open window was inky black and clear. Nico lay on his back and stared out at the night, knowing that he would remember this night for the rest of his life. He had never thought that he would fall in love but he had been wrong. Tonight he had fallen in love with Amy, if he hadn't been in love with her already.

Sighing, he turned to look at her lying curled up, fast asleep, at his side and felt his heart ache. Had he been in love with her nine years ago? He wasn't sure. He had been so focused on carrying out his plan to prove himself that he had been deaf, dumb and blind to everything else.

He had refused to acknowledge his own emotions, refused to accept that he had any feelings at all. He had been set on making a success of his life and everything else had been pushed aside. Even Amy and their children. The one she had lost as well as the one she had given birth to. His son. Jacob. How could he ever make up for what he had done? How could she ever forgive him enough to trust him? Should he even expect her to when he wasn't sure if he could live up to the role of being Jacob's father?

Panic assailed him and he closed his eyes, trying his best to contain it. While he wanted to be a proper father to Jacob, and wanted it desperately too, was he fit to take on the responsibility? Oh, it wasn't only the issue of his health, although that was a major factor, obviously. It was his own upbringing that worried him most of all. He had no role model to refer to, no wonderful childhood memories of him and his father enjoying time together. His father had had no interest in him and he had made it perfectly clear too. He had mentioned family genes tonight and although he had been joking about Jacob's apparent liking for the same things he liked, what if he had inherited *his* father's genes and turned out exactly like him? He couldn't bear to think that he would ruin Jacob's life.

'Regrets already?'

Nico sighed when he realised that Amy was awake and watching him. Whilst he wanted to spare her any more pain, he knew that he couldn't lie. 'Doubts more than regrets.'

'Because we slept together?' she said quietly.

'No. I neither regret what we've done nor have doubts about it.'

He dropped a kiss on her mouth, forcing himself to draw back when he felt the familiar tug of desire flare inside him. This wasn't the time to think about making love to her again even if it was what he wanted more than anything. The thought of burying all his fears while she was in his arms was so very tempting but Nico knew he had to resist. It was too important that he got this right. Too important to Jacob and his son's future happiness.

'Then what's wrong? Obviously something is troubling you, Nico.'

There was the faintest tremor in her voice, a reflection of her uncertainty, and Nico silently cursed himself for causing her more distress. Even though he intended to resist temptation, he couldn't stop himself as he pulled her into his arms and cradled her against him.

'I'm afraid that I won't be able to be a proper father to Jacob,' he told her honestly, although it wasn't easy to bare his soul like this. He had told no one about his unhappy childhood. It had never been a topic for discussion. Why, even he and his sister rarely spoke about their father, both of them preferring not to dwell on the negative aspects of their upbringing. To come out and actually admit how unhappy he had been made him feel incredibly vulnerable but Amy deserved to know the truth and have all the facts laid before her before she made her decision.

'I understand how daunting it must be for you, Nico—' she began but he didn't let her finish.

'It is. Although probably not for the reasons you imagine.' He took a quick breath but now that he had started, he needed to continue. 'I never told you about my father, mainly because there is very little to say. To put it bluntly, he is a cold and ruthless man who cared nothing for me and my sister when we were children. He never showed us any affection or even interest. The only thing he is interested in is making money and he has dedicated his life to doing that.'

'And you're worried in case you behave the same towards Jacob?' she guessed astutely and shook her head. 'No. That's ridiculous, Nico. Why, I've watched you with him and you're great—kind, caring, *supportive*.'

'But it's early days,' he countered, wanting her to listen to what he was saying. Maybe she didn't want to believe it but she had to face the facts. And the facts pointed towards him turning out the same way as Christos Leonides had done.

After all, he had never wanted children, had he? In fact, he had taken great care to avoid having any. Surely that was proof that he was very much his father's son.

The thought sent an ice-cold chill through him but he forced himself to carry on. 'It could turn out to be a sort of...well...knee-jerk reaction to finding out that I'm a father. Once I get accustomed to the idea then who knows what will happen?'

'You're going to turn into the proverbial Jekyll and Hyde character?' she scoffed. 'No. I am not buying that, Nico. It's ridiculous!'

'Why? We were only talking about the effect genes can have on a person earlier tonight, so why is it ridiculous? What if I have inherited my father's genes and find that I can't love Jacob as he deserves to be loved?'

'You honestly think that could happen? Or is it merely an excuse you've come up with?'

'An excuse?' he repeated uncertainly.

'Yes!' She sat up and even though the room

was dark he could see the contempt on her face. 'You've got cold feet, haven't you, Nico? You've suddenly realised that if you do take on the role of being Jacob's father it's going to change your whole life and you're not sure if you like the idea.'

'It isn't that,' he said quickly but she refused to listen to him. Tossing back the sheet she climbed out of bed and picked up her clothes, and began dragging them on.

'Don't bother. I understand, Nico. Really I do. I'm only glad that we got this sorted out before Jacob became involved.'

She swept out of the room without another word. Nico leapt out of bed and went to follow her then stopped. What could he say? He couldn't swear that he would be there for Jacob for ever and ever, could he? Even if it did turn out that he wasn't anything like his own father, there was his health to consider. Although he felt perfectly fit and hoped to remain that way, he couldn't make any promises. Having suffered one heart attack, his chances of having another one were increased. Oh, he was religious about taking his medication and leading a healthy life-style but there was no guarantee it wouldn't happen. How would it affect Jacob if he was taken ill or possibly died if they had forged a close father-and-son bond?

Nico sank down onto the bed, overwhelmed by a feeling of despair as he was forced to face the truth. Not only would he have to let Jacob go but he would have to let Amy go as well.

The road was finally reopened shortly before midday. As soon as the phone call came from the clinic to tell Nico that the road was clear, Amy gathered together her and Jacob's belongings and carried them out to the car. She felt strangely removed from what was happening but she knew it wouldn't last. At some point soon the full impact of what had happened that morning would hit her.

'Have you got everything?'

'Yes.'

Nico opened the car door for her and Amy slid into the seat, barely glancing at him as she fastened her seat belt. By tacit consent they had avoided one another since that discussion in his bedroom. Quite frankly, Amy had nothing to say to him, not now that he had made his position so very clear. Nico had rejected the idea of playing any part in Jacob's life and by doing so he had also rejected her. It was a repeat of what had happened nine years ago so she shouldn't have felt surprised or hurt but she did.

Tears stung her eyes as she placed her bag in the footwell but she blinked them away as Jacob scrambled into the back. There was no way that she wanted Jacob to know what had happened, no way at all that she would allow him to be hurt. It would be far better if Jacob never learned the truth about Nico rather than discover that his father didn't want him.

'I wish we could stay. We could go to the caves again this afternoon, couldn't we, Nico?' Jacob exhorted, glancing hopefully up at Nico who was fastening his seat belt.

'I'm afraid not.'

Nico's voice was even but Amy could hear a thread of something beneath the carefully level tones. Was he feeling uncomfortable? she wondered. Feeling guilty perhaps about rejecting his own flesh and blood? She sighed, realising that she was attributing to him emotions he didn't possess. Nico had had no difficulty rejecting her and their child nine years ago so why should she imagine that he had any qualms about doing so again?

'I have to go to the clinic so I shall be busy for the rest of the day. I am sure that your mother will take you to the beach or think of something exciting you can do instead.'

'S'pose so,' Jacob muttered, obviously not enthralled by the idea. He suddenly brightened. 'What about tonight? You won't have to be at the clinic then, will you, Nico?'

'No. Nico is extremely busy and can't spend all

his time entertaining us.' Amy held up her hand when Jacob opened his mouth to protest. 'I said no, Jacob, and that's the end of it.'

Jacob sank back in his seat, obviously realising that he wasn't going to win this particular argument. Amy swung round and faced the front as Nico closed the rear door. The sooner they were back at the hotel, the better. There were just a few days of their holiday left and then she and Jacob could leave the island and forget all about what had happened here...

'I'm sorry. I've made a complete mess of everything, haven't I?'

Nico's voice was low so that Jacob couldn't overhear what he was saying but she still flinched. She shot a glance at him then turned and stared through the windscreen again, not wanting anything to pierce the cocoon of numbness that enveloped her. It would be a mistake to imagine that his apology was genuine, that he cared. The only person Nico cared about was himself.

Thankfully, he didn't say anything else as he drove them back to the hotel. Maybe he had realised that it would be a waste of time to dredge up any more meaningless excuses. He drew up outside the front door, not bothering to switch off the engine as he turned to her. 'I hope you don't mind if I don't come in with you. It's bound to be busy at the clinic with appointments having been disrupted and I need to go straight there.'

'Of course.' Amy opened the car door and went to get out, pausing when Nico placed his hand on her arm. Even though he only held her lightly, she could feel the imprint of his fingers burning into her skin and bit her lip when desire surged through her once more. She couldn't afford to feel this way. Nico wasn't going to be part of her life from this point on and she had to forget about him.

'I'm sorry, Amy. Truly I am.'

There was nothing she could say, nothing that would help to alleviate the pain of being rejected a second time. Amy shook off his hand and got out of the car then helped Jacob out of the back. Nico bent forward to look at them and there was such anguish in his eyes that she almost weakened, almost but not quite. If he had felt anything—really felt anything—then he couldn't have turned his back on their son or on her.

Amy turned away, taking hold of Jacob's hand as they mounted the steps to the front door. She heard the car engine rev to life followed by the crunch of tyres on gravel as Nico drove away but she didn't stop or look back. There was no point. Nico had gone from her life a second time. And this time she would make sure he never came back.

CHAPTER FOURTEEN

TIME PASSED IN a blur. Although Nico did everything that was expected of him, it felt as though he was functioning at one step removed. He was haunted by the memory of how Amy had looked when he had left her at the hotel. Several times he was tempted to go to see her and try to explain why he felt it was better that he didn't get involved in Jacob's life but somehow he managed to resist. Even if she believed him, it wouldn't change anything. The truth was that Jacob would be better off without him. All he would be doing was applying a little salve to his own conscience.

The day when Amy and Jacob were due to leave the island rolled around. Nico knew they would need to take the ferry back to the mainland so they could catch their flight. Jacob had mentioned that they were flying home in the dark so he guessed they would catch the noon ferry from Constantis. He busied himself with the clinic's affairs then emailed a former colleague who now worked in Athens. He intended to go ahead with his plan to utilise his skills by working in reconstructive surgery. Apart from the fact that he wanted to do it, it would give him something to focus on. He couldn't bear to imagine that he would live out the rest of his days feeling the way he did at this moment—empty and desolate. Concentrating on the demands of such a taxing job would help to fill the gap in his life. *Hopefully.*

Amy had packed their cases the night before so there was very little to do on their last day on the island. She took Jacob to breakfast, only half listening as he chattered away. It was three days since she had seen Nico, three days that she had spent missing him every hour and every minute and every second. Even when she finally fell asleep at night, he was there in her head, smiling down at her in the moments before they had made love. It was as though the intervening years had never happened and she was right back where she had been: aching and hurt, her heart broken at being rejected. It was hard to maintain a happy front for Jacob's benefit but she refused to do anything that might upset him.

Donna Roberts and her family were already in the dining room when Amy arrived. She was poking the figs, piercing their skins with her bright orange fingernails. She pulled a face when Amy joined her at the buffet table.

'I'll be glad to get back home to some proper food. I mean, who wants stuff like this for breakfast? My Harvey is dying for a bowl of his favourite choco-pops!'

Amy merely smiled, not wanting to be drawn into a discussion about the merits of Donna's children's usual diet. She selected a couple of ripe figs and filled a bowl with yogurt then reached for the bread basket.

'It's all right for you. Your kid probably enjoys this sort of food 'cos he's used to it.'

'I'm sorry?' Amy glanced uncertainly at the woman, unsure what she meant by the comment.

''Cos he's Greek. Well, part Greek, anyway. He's that Dr Leonides's kid, isn't he?' Donna didn't wait for Amy to answer. 'They're the spitting image of one another, aren't they? There's no way the doc can claim not to be his dad when they're like two peas in a pod!'

Amy had no idea what to say. Picking up her tray, she hurriedly carried it over to their table but her hands were shaking as she unloaded it. The thought of how easily the truth could have come out if Donna had said anything in Jacob's hearing gave her hot and cold chills but she forced herself to sit down and eat her breakfast as though nothing had happened. The last thing she must do was panic. She just needed to get through another couple of hours and then they could leave the island for good.

Amy took Jacob to the beach after breakfast, wanting to fill in the time before they were due to catch the ferry. She had been intending to travel into town on the local bus but decided to order a taxi instead. A couple of times the bus had failed to turn up because of engine trouble and she didn't want anything going wrong and delaying them. Leaving Constantis was her main priority. Once they had left the island then she might be able to put what had happened into some sort of perspective. She sighed, realising that it was wishful thinking. The repercussions from this holiday were going to stay with her for a very long time.

She stopped at the desk on their way to the beach and asked Helena for the number of a local taxi firm. Helena immediately offered to make the call for her and arranged for her and Jacob to be collected at eleven thirty. Helena shook her head when Amy thanked her for her help and also for their stay at the hotel.

'It has been our pleasure to have you here. Philo and I hope that you will come back again to see us very soon.'

Amy managed to smile but she could feel her

throat closing up with tears. She wouldn't come back to Constantis, not while Nico was here. Even though he had merely lived up to her expectations of him, she couldn't bear to see him again and suffer another rejection. At some point the time would come when she would have to tell Jacob the truth but not right now. Not while she felt so hurt and so wounded. No, a few years down the line she would be able to explain the situation to Jacob with equanimity. She would lay out her reasons for keeping Nico's identity a secret, and also explain Nico's reasons for wanting her to keep it to herself. When Jacob was older, he would be better able to understand the complexities of the situation. Or she hoped he would.

Amy collected Jacob, who was playing in the garden, and took him to the beach for a final swim before they left. And if her heart was full of dread at the thought of what lay ahead at some point in the future then she tried not to dwell on it. Nico had made it clear that he wanted nothing to do with their son so she had no choice in the matter. She had to focus on the fact that Jacob would be better off without a father rather than have someone in his life who didn't care about him.

Nico had had absolutely no intention of going to see Amy before she and Jacob left. He had said all he had to say and even though he found it almost unbearable, he had to stick to his decision. Jacob would be better off without him and Amy would be too. They could get on with their lives and look towards the future.

Who was to say that Amy wouldn't meet someone and fall in love? Now that he thought about it, he was surprised it hadn't happened already. She was so beautiful and kind, so sweet and generous that he would have expected her to have been snapped up by some lucky guy, but from what he could gather there didn't appear to be anyone on the scene, no boyfriend or lover, although maybe he was mistaken about that. After all, why would she discuss her love life with him? Even if they had slept together? There could be someone back in England waiting to welcome her home.

The thought ate away at him all morning long despite the fact that they were even busier than usual. An outbreak of food poisoning at one of the larger hotels along the coast resulted in numerous calls for assistance. As most of the people involved were in no fit state to travel to the surgery, Nico offered to drive to the hotel and visit them in their rooms. He took Sophia with him and was glad he had done as several more guests had presented with the same symptoms. All in all, there were thirty-three people suffering from sickness and diarrhoea and he wouldn't be surprised if there were many more before the end of the day. A bug like this could quickly run riot.

Nico worked his way through the list of people, offering advice as well as handing out sachets of rehydration medication. Sickness and diarrhoea soon caused dehydration and the very young as well as the very old and infirm were most at risk. Fortunately, they had picked up supplies on the way but even so they barely had enough for everyone. Nico wrote out a prescription and handed it to the hotel's manager then explained that he would need to report the incident to the relevant authorities. Checks would need to be made on the hotel's kitchens to find the source of the outbreak.

It was well after three by the time he and Sophia arrived back at the clinic. Nico parked his car and thanked Sophia for her help then sent her home. She had been due to take the afternoon off and he appreciated the fact that she had offered to go with him. There was an antenatal clinic that day but as Elena was taking it, he was free to leave as well, but he went to his office first and phoned the local health inspector and explained what had happened. It was almost half past the hour by the time that was done and he sighed as he got up to leave. If nothing else, the incident had stopped him going after Amy. The ferry would have docked by now and she and Jacob would be on their way to the airport. One thing was certain: they wouldn't come back again.

The thought hung heavily over him as he made his way to Reception. Theodora was manning the desk and she handed him a couple of messages that had come while he was out. Nico glanced through them as he left but there was nothing urgent that couldn't wait until tomorrow...

'Nico! Is he here?'

Nico looked up, his heart surging when he saw Amy running up the drive towards him. She was out of breath when she reached him and he caught hold of her arm and steadied her.

'What is it? What's happened?' he demanded.

'It's Jacob. I can't find him. He's disappeared.'

She was gasping for air, panic making it even more difficult for her to speak. Nico led her back inside to his office and sat her down then crouched in front of her. 'Tell me what happened, right from the beginning,' he instructed, trying to stay calm, not an easy task when his heart was hammering with fear.

'I booked a taxi to bring us into town so we could catch the ferry,' Amy explained. 'There's been a few occasions recently when the bus hasn't turned up and I didn't want to risk it happening again today.'

Nico nodded, refusing to dwell on her reasons for wanting to ensure their departure went smoothly. He couldn't blame her if she was anxious to leave the island after what he had told her. 'So you took a taxi. Then what happened?'

'The taxi was late collecting us so we had to rush when we reached the harbour. Most of the passengers had already boarded the ferry so I told Jacob to stay close to me and ran up the gangplank with our suitcase.' She had to pause to drag in some more air and Nico took hold of her hand and gently squeezed it.

'Take your time, Amy. I know how hard this is but I need to know exactly what happened.'

'Of course.' She took another shaky breath.

'There were several other latecomers as well as us and it was chaotic as everyone tried to get on board at once. I looked round to make sure that Jacob was all right and spotted him at the bottom of the gangplank. I just assumed he was following me but when I got on deck I couldn't see him.'

Tears began to run down her cheeks. 'I looked everywhere, Nico, asked people if they had seen him, did everything I could think of, but there was no sign of him on board the boat. The crew helped me look but they couldn't find him either. The ferry had set sail by the time we had finished checking every conceivable hiding place and the captain explained that he couldn't turn back.' She gulped. 'I had to travel all the way to Athens then come back here on the same boat. I was hoping that Jacob would be waiting at the harbour but he wasn't there and no one has seen him.'

She clutched his hand, her nails digging into his skin as panic overwhelmed her. 'Where is he, Nico? What's happened to him?'

CHAPTER FIFTEEN

AMY CLOSED HER eyes and tried to calm herself as Nico saw the police officer out. There were just a handful of police officers on the island but they had promised to start searching for Jacob immediately. As the officer had said in a bid to reassure her, he couldn't have gone very far because the island was so small. He would soon turn up, the policeman had stated confidently, and she hoped and prayed he was right. She would never forgive herself if anything had happened to him.

'They will phone me when they find him.'

Nico came back into his office, his handsome face etched with the same concern that must be on hers. That he was worried about their son wasn't in any doubt and it surprised her. Why should Nico care so much when he wanted nothing to do with Jacob?

'*If* they find him,' she murmured, too upset to delve into the reason why.

'We will find him, Amy.' He swung round and she could tell from the tension that gripped him the battle he was having to maintain his control. Nico cared; he really cared. It made his decision not to play any part in Jacob's life all the more difficult to understand... Unless it was the thought of having to be around her that had been the deciding factor? Nico might want to be a father to their son but it didn't mean he wanted to become involved with her.

The thought was just too much on top of everything else that had happened. A sob welled from her lips then another and another. It was as though a dam had burst and all the pain and disillusionment that had built up in the past few days came flooding out. Nico crossed the room in a couple of long strides and knelt in front of her but she resisted when he tried to take her in his arms. She didn't want his pity! She didn't want anything at all from him when it was only being offered out of a sense of duty.

'No!' She pushed him away and leapt to her feet, almost overturning the chair in her haste. 'I don't need you consoling me, Nico. I know how you feel about me so let's not pretend.'

'How I feel?'

'Yes. I'm nothing more than a nuisance as far as you are concerned. Not only did I give birth to a chid you never wanted but I had the audacity to turn up here and disrupt your life all over again.' She gave a bitter laugh. 'Maybe you could have accepted Jacob as your son but not if it meant having to see me as well. That was way too much for you to put up with, wasn't it? No wonder you decided that you wanted nothing more to do with us.'

'You're wrong. So wrong that it would be laughable if it weren't so insulting.'

He rounded on her, his eyes blazing with anger, and Amy took an instinctive step back. He didn't follow her, however, just stood there, glaring at her with undisguised contempt as well as something else, something that made her racing heart beat even faster. To see such anguish in his eyes was a shock, especially when she had no idea what had caused it.

'I didn't decide not to become involved in Jacob's life because of you, Amy. On the contrary, it was one of the biggest inducements of all. I had to constantly remind myself that it was Jacob's well-being that mattered and not what *I* wanted.'

'What you wanted?' she said, feeling dizzy from the rush of blood that was surging through her veins. It took her all her time to concentrate when her thoughts seemed to be swirling around. 'I don't understand. What exactly do you want, Nico?'

'You.'

Nico closed the gap between them, praying that he wasn't about to make matters worse, but the time for pretence was over. He had to tell Amy the truth about how he felt and if it wasn't what she wanted to hear then so be it. His voice grated as he continued but that was only to be expected when it was the first time he had opened his heart and laid himself bare. 'I want you, Amy. I want you so much it hurts but I won't run the risk of hurting Jacob.'

'You want me?'

Her voice was the merest whisper and he sighed, understanding her confusion. Why should she believe him after the way he had behaved? He had rejected her, not once but twice, after all. He caught hold of her hands, willing her to believe what he was saying or at least not pour scorn on his declaration.

'Yes. I love you, Amy. I realised it when we spent that night together, although I think I was probably in love with you way before then only I wasn't ready to admit it.'

'I don't know what to say…' She tailed off, her eyes huge and luminous as they stared into his, searching for the truth.

'You don't have to say anything.' He gave her

hands a gentle squeeze then let her go. It would be unfair to press her for a response when their main concern had to be finding Jacob, even more unfair to hope that she might feel something for him too. He didn't deserve her love after the way he had behaved. 'Right now we need to focus on finding Jacob. How did he seem today? Was he his usual self or was he behaving differently in some way?'

'I'm not sure.'

Amy made an obvious effort to collect herself but he heard the tremor in her voice and knew that his declaration had been a shock for her. And the fact that she hadn't suspected how he felt seemed to confirm that she didn't love him. If she had loved him then surely she would have realised how he felt about her?

'Was he excited about going home to see his friends?' he asked, trying to squash that unhappy thought.

'He was first thing this morning but now that I

think about it, he seemed unusually quiet when we got back from the beach.'

'And nothing happened while you were there? You didn't tell him off for instance about doing something he shouldn't?'

'No, not at all. We had a swim then he played with the Roberts children for a while.' She shrugged. 'He just seemed a bit subdued when we went back to the hotel to have a shower before we caught the ferry.'

'I see. Why did you think he might be here?'

She sighed. 'Because he's asked umpteen times when were we going to see you again. Even this morning, when we were in the taxi on our way to the ferry, he asked about you and if you were at the clinic today.' She shrugged. 'I told him that you probably were but it was too late to call in and see you.'

'So it's possible that he may have come here looking for me,' Nico said slowly, his heart aching at the thought of Jacob wanting to prolong contact with him. Had he been right to rule himself out of the child's life? He had thought he was doing the right thing but he was no longer certain any more.

'It's possible, I suppose. But you would have seen him if he had come here, wouldn't you?'

'I might not have done.' He quickly explained about the outbreak of food poisoning at the hotel. 'Jacob could have assumed I wasn't here today when he didn't see my car parked outside.'

'So he probably wouldn't have come in,' Amy said slowly. She looked at Nico. 'You don't think he would have tried to find his way to your house, do you? I mean, it's a long way and he doesn't know the roads around here all that well.'

'I think it's a possibility and definitely worth checking out.' Nico snatched up the phone and rang the police station, quickly explaining their suspicions. He hung up after the officer promised to send a car to his house to see if Jacob was there. Picking up his keys, he slipped his arm around Amy and hurried her to the door. 'We'll drive straight there and hope we find him sitting on the doorstep.'

'I hope so.' Her voice was choked with emotion and Nico acted instinctively as he held her close for a moment while he planted a gentle kiss on her forehead.

'We'll find him, Amy. I promise you we will.'

He let her go and hurried her outside, pausing only briefly to ask Theodora to phone him immediately if a young boy came into the clinic and asked for him. It seemed unlikely that Jacob would turn up there again if he had been there earlier in the day but he wanted to cover all bases. He sighed as he started the car. Sometimes it did more harm than good to over-think a problem. If he had gone with his gut instinct then none of this might have happened. He would never have told Amy that he didn't want anything more to do with Jacob and when they found him he intended to rectify matters.

If Amy would let him.

Amy sat on the edge of her seat as Nico drove them to his home. Let Jacob be there, she prayed, clinging tight hold to the hope that somehow he had found his way there. However, as the miles passed she realised what a long shot it was. Jacob was only eight and there was no way that he could have walked all this way even if he had remembered which direction to take.

'I can't see him managing to walk this far.'

Amy's heart turned over when Nico voiced her fears. 'Neither can I but where else could he have gone? I mean, he doesn't know that many places, just the hotel and your house...'

'And the caves!' Nico exclaimed. 'He knows that I sometimes go there on my day off so do you think he might have gone there to find me when my car wasn't parked outside the clinic?'

'I don't know. Maybe.'

'It's worth checking. The caves are on our way so we may as well try there first.'

Nico swung the car down a side road, bumping over the uneven ground as he drove at some speed towards the bay. He drew up and got out then ran to the edge of the cliff where the path led down to the cove. Amy hurriedly followed him, shading her eyes as she searched the ground below where they were standing. Her breath caught when she spotted a patch of red half-hidden in the undergrowth on a narrow ledge to the left of the path.

'Look! Over there. That patch of red. Jacob was wearing a red T-shirt today.'

'I see it.'

Nico didn't hesitate as he plunged down the steep path. Rocks skittered from under his feet but he ignored the danger as made his way down. Amy's breath caught as she watched him step off the path and start to make his way over to the ledge. The cliff face had sheared away at this point and there was nothing to stop him if he fell. He made it safely to the ledge and she gasped when he parted the bushes and she saw Jacob lying on the ground. She started to make her own way down the path, stopping when Nico shouted up to her.

'He's breathing but he's unconscious. Can you

go back to the car and phone the clinic? We need an ambulance here as quickly as possible.'

Amy turned round and ran back to the car. The number for the clinic was already logged into Nico's phone and she had no difficulty contacting them. She quickly explained what had happened and was relieved when the receptionist told her that an ambulance would set off immediately.

'It's on its way,' she told Nico as she went back to the head of the path.

'Good.' He looked up and she could see the worry in his eyes. 'I think he may have hit his head when he fell. He needs a CT scan to check what damage has been done.'

'Can you do that at the clinic?' she asked anxiously.

'No. We don't have that facility so he will need to go to the mainland.'

'He will be all right, though, Nico, won't he?' Amy pleaded. She glanced round, trying to work out how she could get down to them. Nico must have realised what she was intending to do because he shook his head.

'You stay there. There isn't room for both of us on this ledge—it's far too narrow. It doesn't feel that stable either and I don't want to risk it breaking away.'

Amy shivered as she glanced at the sheer drop below them. Nico and Jacob wouldn't stand a chance if the ledge gave way. It seemed like a lifetime passed before the sound of an ambulance siren cut through the noise of the waves pounding ashore. Amy went to meet the paramedics, quickly explaining the situation as she led them to the path. The police arrived a few minutes later along with several local men who were kitted out with ropes and harnesses. In a remarkably short time the rescue operation was underway.

Jacob was brought up first, securely strapped to a stretcher that was winched carefully up the cliff face. He looked so small and defenceless that Amy couldn't contain her tears as she bent over and kissed his cheek. His eyelids fluttered as he opened his eyes and looked at her in confusion.

'Mum...'

'It's all right, darling. You're safe now. We're going to take you to the hospital and make sure you're all right.'

'Is Nico here?' He tried to sit up but she stopped him. Until they knew exactly what damage he had done to himself, he mustn't be allowed to move.

'Yes. He'll be here in a second. The men are just helping him up the cliff... Oh, here he is now.'

Amy moved aside as Nico came to join them. His face was grey with a combination of fear and fatigue but he managed to smile as he crouched down beside Jacob.

'So you're awake. How do you feel?'

'My head hurts,' Jacob muttered before his eyes closed again.

Nico didn't waste any more time as he told the

ambulance crew to load the stretcher on board. He helped Amy into the back. 'I'll go on ahead and make arrangements to have Jacob moved to the mainland. The sooner we get him there, the happier I'll be.'

'It's still over an hour by boat,' she said anxiously.

'Which is why I propose to have him transferred by helicopter.' He bent and kissed her on the mouth. 'He will be all right, Amy. I shall do everything in my power to make sure he is.'

Amy wanted to believe him; she wanted it more than anything but she knew just how serious the situation was. She sat down as the crew closed the ambulance doors and her last sight of Nico was the anxiety on his face as he ran over to his car. It wasn't just professional concern for a patient either. It was the deep, gut-wrenching fear a parent felt for their child. She knew then that she had been wrong to doubt Nico, that *he* had been wrong to doubt himself. He loved Jacob and loved him as a father should. And it was a love that would last a lifetime too if it had the chance.

The CT scan showed a bleed on the left side of Jacob's brain. Nico tried to maintain the necessary professional detachment as he and the consultant studied the monitor but his heart was pounding. If left untreated the build-up of pressure inside the child's skull could become life-threatening so it needed to be dealt with immediately.

He thanked the other man and went to find Amy who was in the waiting room. She leapt to her feet when he appeared and he saw the fear on her face. The fact that he was about to add to it made him feel doubly wretched but there was nothing he could do. He led her back to a chair and sat her down.

'There's a small bleed on the left side of Jacob's brain,' he told her quietly, knowing that he didn't need to explain how serious the situation was. As an experienced trauma nurse she understood only too well the implications of such an injury.

'Oh!' She pressed her hand to her mouth and Nico sighed.

'I know. But at least we know it's there and they can deal with it. The fact that we got Jacob to hospital so quickly will also go in his favour.'

'Where did you manage to find a helicopter at such short notice?' Amy asked, dabbing away the tears that had welled to her eyes.

'I phoned my father and asked him if we could use his,' he explained shortly. It was the first time he had asked Christos Leonides for anything since he had grown up but it had been essential that they got Jacob to the hospital as quickly as possible. In the event his father had come up trumps: not only had he sent his helicopter but he had arranged for Jacob to be flown straight to the main hospital in Athens where he could be seen by one of Greece's leading neurosurgeons. Nico was aware that he owed Christos a debt of gratitude but decided that he would worry about that later.

'Thank heavens he agreed!' Amy exclaimed,

clutching hold of his hand. 'So what happens now? Are they going to operate?'

'Yes. Jacob is being prepared even as we speak so it shouldn't be long before he's in Theatre. I had a word with the surgeon and he is quietly optimistic, although there are no guarantees at this stage.' His voice broke and he couldn't continue as fear for his son overwhelmed him once more.

'He will get through this, Nico. I'm sure about that.'

Amy leant forward and hugged him while Nico tried to get a grip on his emotions. He drew back and sighed, feeling worse than ever about not being able to offer her the reassurance she needed so desperately.

'He will.' He stood up, unable to sit there while Jacob was in such danger. 'I think I shall go and have a word with the theatre sister if you don't mind.'

'You do that.' Amy smiled bravely up at him. 'You concentrate on our son, Nico. I'll be here waiting.'

Nico felt his heart surge as he left the room. Maybe they hadn't worked out the details but he knew that he and Amy would find a way to resolve any issues. It was too important that they did; important to Jacob and important to them as well. If they were to become a family then they had to start behaving as one. If being a family was what Amy wanted.

A tiny doubt flew into his mind but he swatted it away. He made his way to Theatre and spoke to the sister in charge, deriving comfort from her assurance that the surgeon who was carrying out the procedure was highly skilled. He went back to the waiting room, taking hold of Amy's hand and holding it tightly as the minutes ticked past. Now it was a waiting game. All they could do was wait and pray that Jacob responded to the treatment.

Amy was exhausted by the time morning came. She and Nico had spent the night at Jacob's bedside. Nico had tried to persuade her to go to the parents' room and rest but she had refused. She needed to be there when Jacob woke up. She looked up when a nurse came to check Jacob's obs again. Nico had explained that the surgeon planned to keep Jacob sedated to allow his brain time to heal. There was a degree of swelling and it would help his recovery. Amy knew it was standard procedure but she couldn't help wishing that Jacob would open his eyes so that she would know he was all right. Having to wait like this was almost unbearable.

The nurse finished her task, smiling sympathetically at them before she left. All the staff had been wonderful, going out of their way to make sure that they had everything they needed. It was obvious that they knew Jacob was Nico's son and she found herself wondering if Nico had told them or if they had worked it out for themselves, not that it mattered. The only thing that mattered was that Jacob should recover. Tears stung her eyes once more and she blinked them away. Nico put down the chart and reached across the bed to squeeze her hand.

'He's doing well, Amy. His obs are fine and he is more than holding his own.'

'Good.' She managed a watery smile. 'I never realised how stressful it is keeping watch like this. Your mind starts conjuring up all kinds of awful scenarios.'

'It does. But I have a feeling there is going to be a happy ending from this. Hopefully, for all of us.'

'You've changed your mind about wanting to be involved in Jacob's life,' she said simply. It wasn't a question when she already knew the answer.

'It's what I've wanted for a while now. If you will agree, of course, and I wouldn't blame you if you weren't happy with the idea.'

'I am. It's what I want more than anything, Nico, but only if you're sure it's what you want.'

'I can't think of anything I have ever wanted more.' His eyes held hers. 'I want to be a proper father to Jacob and be part of his life. I also want to be part of your life, Amy, if you will allow me to be.'

'It's what I want too. More than anything.'

'Darling!' Nico got up and came around the bed. He drew her to her feet and held her tightly against him so that she could feel the heavy beat of his heart echoing through her body. 'I can hardly believe that you are willing to give me another chance after the way I hurt you. I would do anything to make up for what I did nine years ago, my love. Anything in the whole world!'

'You've already done it.' She smiled up at him, loving him more than ever at that moment. That Nico was telling her the truth wasn't in doubt and her heart overflowed with happiness. 'You've accepted Jacob as your son and I know that you will come to love him as much as I do. That's more than enough.'

'I don't deserve you.' He kissed her hungrily, his lips seeking a response she was only too willing to give. He sighed as he drew back. 'My only concern now is my health and the impact it could have on you and Jacob if I was to have another heart attack. I can't bear to think of you two suffering because of me.'

'Don't.' She placed her fingers against his lips. 'There's no point worrying about something that may never happen. All right, so maybe you are at greater risk than other people but you are fit and healthy at this moment and that's what matters.' She glanced at their son. 'We shall concentrate on Jacob getting better and on making plans for our future together.'

'Thank you.' He captured her hand and pressed his lips to her palm. 'Thank you for giving me such a wonderful gift as Jacob and for being you. I am so very lucky, Amy.'

'No, I'm the lucky one,' she murmured.

Two years later...

'Careful!'

Amy ran across the grass and scooped up her daughter before she toppled into the paddling pool. Twelve-month-old Luisa had just learned to walk and loved exploring her surroundings. Amy had only taken her eyes off her for a moment and the little girl had managed to stagger over to the paddling pool.

'It's OK, Mum. I'll look after her.'

Jacob abandoned the game of football he was enjoying with his cousins and came racing over to take his sister from her. Carefully holding her hand, he helped her into the pool and climbed in beside her. Amy smiled when the sound of laughter rang around the garden.

'He's so good with her, isn't he?' Nico came and flopped down on the grass beside her. Having followed through with his plans to return to reconstructive surgery by taking a part-time post at the hospital on the mainland, his days were extremely full. However, he refused to allow work to interfere with their family life and spent as much time as possible with Jacob and Luisa.

Nico had proved himself to be a wonderful father and Amy knew that any doubts he may

286 THE GREEK DOCTOR'S SECRET SON

have had in that respect had disappeared and was glad.

'He is. Jacob really adores her.'

Amy smiled down at him, thinking how lucky she was. She and Nico had been married for almost two years now and they had been the most wonderful years she could have imagined. Jacob had quickly recovered from his injuries and thankfully hadn't suffered any after-effects. As soon as he had been well enough they had told him the truth about Nico being his father, although it hadn't been the surprise they had imagined it would be. It turned out that Harvey Roberts had overheard his parents discussing the fact that Jacob was Nico's son and had told Jacob, which was why Jacob had wanted to find Nico on the day they were due to leave the island. He had been delighted when they had confirmed that it was true which had been a huge relief.

Amy had needed to return to England once Jacob was better to sort out her affairs, but she had soon returned to Constantis. She had taken over from Sophia as senior sister at the clinic and had worked there until she had left to have Luisa. Although her parents had been a little wary when she had told them about Nico, they had soon got over their initial reservations once they had met him. As her father had said, it was obvious how much Nico adored her and Jacob and that was good enough for them. They were coming to stay the following week to spend time with their grandchildren and Amy was looking forward to seeing them, although apart from family and friends, she missed very little of her old life in England, mainly because she had everything she needed right here on the island.

As for Nico's relationship with his father there had been a cautious improvement. Although Christos would never be a doting family man, he had made an effort to maintain contact with them and seemed to enjoy spending time with his grandchildren, albeit for very short periods. Amy knew that it had helped Nico to put the past behind him and concentrate on the future, a future that seemed to be filled with so much promise that sometimes she had to pinch herself to know she wasn't dreaming. Now as Nico bent towards her, she felt her heart spill over with love and gratitude for everything he had given her.

'As I adore you.' Cupping her face in his hands, he kissed her softly and with great tenderness. 'I love you, my darling. Now and for ever.'

'And I love you too. Now and for ever,' she echoed, kissing him back.

* * * * *